Annerton Pit

PETER DICKINSON

Annerton Pit

An Atlantic Monthly Press Book
Little, Brown and Company
BOSTON   TORONTO

FIRST AMERICAN EDITION

T 09/77

Library of Congress Cataloging in Publication Data

Dickinson, Peter, 1927–
  Annerton Pit.

  "An Atlantic Monthly Press book."
  SUMMARY: In search of their grandfather who has disappeared while tracking down ghosts, two brothers, one blind, stumble upon a headquarters of subversive revolutionary activity in an abandoned mine.
  [1. Ghost stories. 2. Blind—Fiction. 3. England —Fiction] I. Title.
PZ7.D562An3   [Fic]   77–9885
ISBN 0-316-18430-6

ATLANTIC–LITTLE, BROWN BOOKS
ARE PUBLISHED BY
LITTLE, BROWN AND COMPANY
IN ASSOCIATION WITH
THE ATLANTIC MONTHLY PRESS

PRINTED IN THE UNITED STATES OF AMERICA

THE POSTMAN was the one who whistled "Amazing Grace" rather well but couldn't manage the flap of the letter box. Jake Bertold heard him stuff something fairly bulky through and then the flap snapped back just as the package hit the doormat. Martin's chair squeaked slightly on the kitchen tiles, but only enough to show that he was rocking himself comfortably back against the fridge, which Mum would never let him do when she was there, so he probably hadn't heard the postman. The flap was rattling again as Jake got up and walked out of the kitchen and up the two steps into the hallway. The snap of the flap was dulled by something the postman hadn't pushed right through.

"Thank you," called Jake as boots and "Amazing Grace" dwindled away into the street. He pulled the letter clear of the flap, just one cheap envelope feeling like a bill. His foot touched the package on the doormat so he bent to pick it up. Martin's *Motorcycle Mechanics* — nothing else came rolled quite like that. He knew that there was no more post on the mat because he'd have heard it fall, but while he was down he couldn't help sweeping a hand around just in case. Nothing. He did his best not to let his feelings show when he carried the post back to the kitchen. Martin was trying to jiggle a crookedly cut bit of bread out of the toaster.

"Here's your comic," said Jake.

"Thanks. This stupid gadget!"

"Why don't you cut the bread straighter? It always works when I do it. One bill, I think."

"Oughtn't to be. Dad said he'd settled everything for the next six weeks. Oh, come on!"

Metal slithered on smooth metal.

"Look out!" said Jake. "You mustn't use a knife. That element's live even when it's stopped toasting. I bet you haven't switched it off!"

"I want my rotten toast."

"Let me do it."

Jake was quite right about Martin having been too impatient to switch the current off. He did so, then turned the toaster on its side and humored the mangled slice free. At least, he thought, it hadn't been as bad as Saturday when he'd come racing downstairs after hearing the unmistakable flutter of a postcard and it had turned out to be only one from Mum and Dad. Martin muttered as he tried to rip the wrapper off his magazine, starting, as happened every month, in the wrong place so that he tore the cover.

"Thanks," he said as he took the toast. "Nothing from Granpa?"

"No."

"You want me to go and look? It might have fallen in a funny place."

"I'd have heard."

"Spect so. I wonder what's happened to the old idiot. He's probably too hot on the trail of some banshee to

❖ 4

remember that he's got any family at all. That's two weeks, isn't it?"

"Yes."

"Honestly, when you get that old I suppose you've got a right to go a bit nutty, but not inconsiderate. He knows Mum and Dad are away, too."

"Something's wrong."

"Oh, come off it."

"I suppose so."

"Why can't they do these things up in wrappers which you don't need a blowtorch to undo. Soon as Granpa's subscription runs out I'm going to start buying it at Smith's again."

"You always start in the wrong place."

"I start where I feel like. It's a free country, isn't it? Ah!"

Jake drank his tea listening to the flop and rattle of pages being leafed to and fro as Martin looked for goodies in the magazine. Then came a sigh of content as his brother settled down to read some article in a sensible fashion, starting at the beginning. The faint mutter of Mrs. Quitch's radio next door died. That meant *Thought for the Day* had begun and she'd switched it off, so it was quarter to eight and time to dress for school. Jake was almost at the door when he heard Martin say in a quite different voice, "Hey, that isn't a bill!" As he went up the stairs he felt the mood of the house change — first a shock wave of excitement and then a violent lurch into fear and depression, something far deeper and more intense than his own fret about not hearing from Granpa. That was only a guess, of course: when Jake had these feelings about the mood of the house he was sometimes wrong, but he was quite often right.

Jake always had breakfast in his dressing gown, a habit

left over from the years when he couldn't help spilling some of his food, and of course Mum wanted to send him clean to school. From habit he also paraded in the kitchen, though nowadays he never contrived to put on odd shoes or wear his jersey inside out.

Martin had turned the radio on for the news as he always did, but he wasn't listening to it. In fact he switched the reader off in the middle of a sentence about the trial of the Green Revolutionary bombers, when normally he'd have insisted on complete silence from the rest of the family so that he could glean every scrap about his heroes. But today he gave a mutter of furious impatience and then *click*.

"You'll do," he said.

Jake was careful not to show that he could hear the bleakness and shock in his voice.

"Thanks," he said. "I — "

"They've turned me down," said Martin with a laugh like the bark of a small dog.

"Who have?"

"All three universities I put in for. Oh, God, if only I'd done a bit of work I could have got in on my head! They're crying out for engineers! I've been such a fool!"

"I'm sorry."

"Oh, God!"

Jake didn't know what to say. He made a beginning in his mind and then stopped. Really, they'd all known this was going to happen. Martin *hadn't* done a lot of work, and even Granpa, who practically never commented on anyone else's behavior, had once been heard muttering that nobody had ever built a bridge with nothing but flair and flannel. Martin had laughed. But that was then. And since then he'd managed to drive the coming crisis out of his mind by joining in all the student marching and protesting and fund raising over the GR bombers' trial.

Mr. Scott's hooter pooped outside the front gate.

"I've got to go," said Jake. "It'll be all right, Mart — it really will."

"Couldn't you cut school? I can't face being alone all day — nothing to do but clean the rotten house and pretend to work for my rotten A-levels which I don't need any more and listen to those prissy-voweled news readers talking about the trial and think. Say I've got flu or something and you've got to look after me."

"Oh . . . OK," said Jake.

He walked rapidly down the hallway and picked up his stick from its corner among the coats and macs. When he opened the door he left it on the latch. He smelled the remains of rain in the March air, though the sound of the passing tires on the road told him that the tarmac was almost dry. A soft wind on his cheek felt as though it would soon rain again.

"Fraid I'm early," called Mr. Scott's furry voice. "Got a bit of a rush on this morning. Can you hurry?"

Jake walked down the path, took three steps across the pavement, and tapped his way past Mr. Quitch's parked car.

"You'll need your anorak," said Mr. Scott. "Forecast's rain all day. And where's your satchel?"

"I think I'd better not come to school," said Jake. "Martin's not very well. I expect it's only flu, but it might be the thing he had before."

"You can't do much," said Mr. Scott.

"Yes I can. I looked after him a lot when he was ill last time. If I think he's getting worse I'll go to Mrs. Quitch and ask her to ring the doctor."

"But what about the school?"

"She'll do that for me too. They won't mind. Miss Chandow doesn't come Mondays so I don't get a proper blind-teacher today anyway. I've got some work I can do at home."

"Sure? Well, in that case . . . Matter of fact it suits me . . . Any news from your parents?"

"They're having a lovely time. Solid sun, Mum says, and beautiful girls for Dad to look at. A lot of them go bathing with no clothes on at all, Mum says."

"You don't say!" said Mr. Scott. "And all that off the back of a cornflake packet! I'll have to change my breakfast habits. If your Dad can win a competition, so can I, hey?"

The end of his sentence was half drowned by the drub of his starter motor. Jake waved good-bye as the suck of wind behind the car riffled through his hair. Funny, he thought. Nobody ever dreams a blind child might be lying.

Martin had retuned to Radio Solent and turned the volume full up. It was the Bay City Rollers and they were too much for the tinny little speaker. Jake could smell that Martin had made himself another cup of coffee, double strength. He reached out his hand to the core of the bawling and twanging, ran his fingertips along the plastic, and turned the volume down.

"Sorry," he said. "That loud they make my teeth ache."

"Stops me thinking," said Martin. "What did he say?"

"Nothing. He was in a hurry to get off somewhere. I'll go round to Mrs. Quitch and ask her to phone the school."

"What'll you tell her?"

"You've got flu, and I've got to stay at home in case it turns out to be the bug you had before."

"But that means I'm stuck here all day! I won't be able to stand that! Couldn't you phone from the call box?"

"I suppose so. Where do you want to go?"

"I haven't thought. I just want out."

Jake didn't say anything — it was so exactly like Martin. First he insisted on Jake staying at home to keep him company, and then he decided to go out. "Out" meant on the moped Granpa had given him, and it didn't have a pillion so he couldn't take Jake with him. Martin wasn't stupid, he was just incredibly impulsive.

"Tell you what," he said suddenly. "If I'm not going to university I won't need that money. I can use it to trade the moped in and get a proper bike. Let's do that!"

"You'd better talk to Dad — "

"It's my money. It wasn't even given me — I earned it, didn't I?"

"Yes, but — "

"It's either that or send it to the GR Defense Fund."

Jake argued a bit more, but there wasn't much he could say. Martin was quite capable of talking himself into a position where he'd feel forced to send the money to the Green Revolutionary lawyers, and if he did that there'd be real trouble when Dad got home.

Not that it was Dad's money. Apart from a few small presents Martin had earned it all during the last four holidays, slogging away at petrol stations or on building sites so that Dad wouldn't have to fork out anything to make up his university grant to enough money for a student to live on. He'd once or twice talked in a daydreamy way about spending it on a real bike, and had even passed his driving test on a big Honda belonging to his friend Brian. Obviously it would be better if he let this dream come true than if he threw the whole lot away on the GR, who probably had plenty of cash rolling in to help them anyway. Dad would understand, even sympathize, about the bike. GR, no. Jake gave up arguing.

9 ❖

"Where's the showrooms?" he said.

"I'll start at Pauling's just behind Woolworth's."

"I could catch the bus down and wait for you on the library steps. Would you mind?"

"Course not. It would mean we could fit you for a crash helmet."

"Me!"

"Come off it. What's the point in me getting a real bike if I can't take you out on it? Next week's half term, isn't it? We'll really go places."

He sounded so excited that anyone who didn't know him would have thought he'd already got over the shock of disappointment, but Jake could sense that it was still there, a hard ball of pain inside him, and the fizz and urgency were his way of wrapping it round with crackling dreams to seal it off and lessen the pain.

The drizzle began while Jake was waiting on the library steps. He tapped his way up them into the shelter of the porch and listened to footsteps and traffic. A moped of the same make as Martin's went by, but with a rattle in its chain which Jake didn't recognize. The third stranger in ten minutes spoke to him.

"You all right, lad?"

The voice of an elderly man, edged with that fuzz of shyness which most people feel when they offer what may be unwanted help.

"Yes, thank you," said Jake. "I'm waiting for my brother."

"OK. Fine. I'll be in the library about twenty minutes and I'll keep an eye open for you when I come out, just in case . . ."

"Thank you so much."

Nice for him, thought Jake. Now he can feel good all

day without having had to do anything at all. He was still grinning when he heard Martin's step and the slight brush and squeak of his leathers.

"Sorry, Jake. Been waiting long?"

"About ten minutes. The bus was a crawler."

"Would be. Anyway there's nothing doing at Pauling's."

"I'd have thought you'd have bought half the shop by now."

"What! Without you to tell me if the man's lying! Mind a bit of a walk?"

"Course not."

Next time the man *was* lying. He took the boys through his new-bike showroom and out by a back door into an echoing shed which smelled of dirty oil and welding gas and damp sacking, where he showed Martin a machine that made him whistle. Jake could hear the immediate note of longing that threaded through his brother's questions. The man was very very sincere, said it took a real rider to manage a beast like that — BSA Thunderbolt 850, 1964, old, yes, but sound workmanship, classic design, cheap because it's a bit more than most fellers care to handle, but you're a big guy, sir — all that. It took him twenty kicks to start the engine, but that was because it hadn't been run for a while. Jake listened to the bellowing surge of the exhaust as he turned the throttle. He cut the engine and waited.

"I thought I'd seen them priced a hundred quid more than that," said Martin, half longing, half in doubt.

"You're thinking of the sixty-five model, sir. And matter of fact if we'd got round to doing a paint job on this we'd have been asking . . ." and so on and so on, very sincere, very helpful.

A shrill bell fizzed.

"That's my front shop, sir," said the man. "My assistant's out. Mind if I leave you a minute to think it over? Start her up again if you want to — nothing wrong with that engine. But don't take her out in the yard. We're not insured for that."

His brisk footsteps echoed away.

"If it's good as he says it's a snip," said Martin.

"How fast will it go?" asked Jake.

"Supposed to do a hundred and thirty, full noise."

"Full noise is right. You'd look pretty silly if you took it to another of your anti-Concorde demos."

"Bikes are different. What do you think?"

"There's something he isn't talking about."

"What do you mean?"

"I don't know. But he's talking so much because there's something he hopes you're not going to ask about."

"Oh . . . sure?"

"About eighty percent."

"Oh . . . he looks you straight in the eyes all the time . . . Um . . . it's dead cheap, of course . . ."

"Isn't it too cheap?"

"Um . . ."

(This was quite a usual sort of conversation between the Bertold brothers. Though Martin was almost eighteen and Jake five years younger they relied on each other a lot. It had begun with Martin as the small hero defending his blind baby brother from the dragons and ogres of the sighted world, but things had evened up since then. Nowadays Martin relied on Jake quite a bit for reading people's moods and feelings — usually their parents', but sometimes even his current girl's. And Jake had found that it was important to let Martin make his own choices and to go along with most of his wild whims; otherwise he simply became extra wild to make up for his brother's caution.)

For a while Martin hummed and grunted and clicked the big machine's controls; then he wheeled it around the shed with its coarse-tread tires making a contented burring on the cement floor. Jake heard the back door of the shop open and close.

"He's coming back," he whispered.

Martin grunted with the effort of lifting the monster back onto its stand. The brisk steps rang once more through the shed.

"Well, sir?" said the man, careful not to sound very interested.

"What's the frame like?" asked Martin.

"Never been in an accident, sir. One owner, never rode her flat out. Quite as good as you could hope for in a bike that age."

That's it, thought Jake. He clicked his tongue several times against his palate, a noise Mum made when Dad was telling one of his honest-to-God stories.

"Well, um . . ." said Martin, still faintly longing. "I don't know . . . I think I'd better look around a bit more."

"Perhaps she is a trifle too big for you, sir," said the man.

Even Martin could hear the needle under the politeness.

"Expect so," he said calmly. "Anyway, I'll look around."

No, Martin wasn't stupid.

That eliminated both the big showrooms near the center of Southampton. Martin went to a phone box, consulted the yellow pages, and rang half a dozen outlying shops. Only one sounded remotely hopeful. He put Jake on a bus and followed it for a mile. When Jake heard the feeble, oddly womanish double hoot of the moped's horn he got off the bus at the next stop and walked, with Martin pushing his moped beside him, down a street where he'd never been. A big blank wall caught all the noises on his left, and on the right little houses with gaps between them sent back confused replies. A strong smell of fresh timber filled the air, backed by a vaguer mixture of odors of rainy earth and old cabbage and wood ash and manure. It was too early in the year for flower smells. Halfway down the street bristle hissed on stone as somebody scrubbed a doorstep.

"It feels a funny sort of area for a bike shop," said Jake.

"I dunno. It's poor but not a slum. Allotments and that. Quite a few people use push-bikes round here, I should think. Anyway, the bloke we're going to see runs a push-bike shop and does motorbikes on the side. I don't know if I want a BMW, though."

"What's that?"

"German bike. Shaft-driven, not chain. Horizontally opposed cylinders — they stick out a bit at the sides but it keeps the weight low. Very reliable. Sort of bike people use for — Here we are. Lovely and crummy."

This shed smelled of lighter grades of oil, and ancient dust, and leather and plastic. Somebody was working near floor level, making metal nudge and click.

"Shall not keep you three seconds," said a man's voice from low down. "I am Mr. Manayev. And you are the young man who was ringing about one of my motorcycles, uh?"

He had a strong foreign accent and sounded elderly, irritable and suspicious. When he got to his feet Jake could tell from the level of his voice that he was very short, too.

"Aha!" he said, evidently noticing Jake's stick for the first time. "And who of you is going to ride the machine, uh?"

He laughed at his joke but Martin took it into his head to hark back to the years of dragons and ogres.

"I bet my brother could if he had to," he snapped.

"I bet," said Mr. Manayev.

"Do you?" said Martin.

"I say so."

"All right," said Jake. "I'm not old enough to ride a motorbike, but if you'll lend me a push-bike I'll bet you ten pence I can ride it along the road and back."

"Come then," said Mr. Manayev. "I am not wanting anyone hurt. I am only making my joke."

"I thought you said you'd bet," said Martin, still angry.

"OK, OK," said Mr. Manayev. "Is an old bike here, which another spill is not hurting. I set the saddle down. You sure you want that, sonny?"

"Ten pence," said Jake.

The long factory wall made it an easy road to ride in; the bike's chain was loose enough to scrape against the guard, and one pedal had a click in it, so Jake didn't need to produce his own noises to set up echoes. He'd just gone past the scrubbing sound when he heard a rush of clawed feet on tarmac and a hysterical yelping close to his left ankle. He wobbled, steadied and wobbled again, almost falling. A woman's voice yelled at the dog just as he got the firmness of wheels beneath him, but by then he was heading straight for the echoes of the barking and there was nothing for it but to carry on with the turn — otherwise he'd have crashed straight into the factory wall. He rode back to the bike shop counting pedal strokes so that he'd know roughly when he'd got there. He braked and felt for the road with a sliding foot.

"You all right, Jake?" said Martin.

"Fine."

"I thought that dog was going to have you off."

"So did I."

"Good," said Mr. Manayev. "Your brother tell me you see nothing at all."

"Not a sausage," said Jake cheerfully.

"Then here is your bet you win. Good. Now we look at a machine, uh?"

The sales ritual was the same, but very different. Mr. Manayev sounded as though he hated the idea of selling his bikes and was angry with Martin for suggesting any such thing. He had three bikes in his garage, all secondhand BMWs, and Jake thought he sounded a bit nutty about them. Two of them would have cost quite a bit more than Martin could afford.

"Why don't you want so much for this one?" asked Martin. "It's the same year."

"Been across the Sahara is why."

"What do you mean?"

"Been. Across. Thee. Sahara," said Mr. Manayev as if speaking to a deaf foreign idiot.

"That's what I was trying to tell you, Jake," said Martin. "If you want to ride a bike across the Sahara you take a BMW."

"Naturally," said Mr. Manayev. "So she has lived hard, but is in good nick, despite. You get three hundred mile to a pint of oil. Not bad, uh?"

The engine started second kick. Mr. Manayev revved and idled it, then let Martin ride it round a bit of waste ground at the back of his yard. The engine had an odd note, not exactly muffled but not strident either.

"At least it's quieter than the other one," said Jake when Martin came back to them.

"Which other one?" snapped Mr. Manayev, bristly with suspicion.

❖ 16

"Oh," said Martin casually, "I was looking at a sixty-four BSA Thunderbolt up at Catch and Catch — "

"I know her," said Mr. Manayev with a yapping laugh. "You not touch her, sonny. Joe Catch, he been trying to sell eight months. Frame twisted like barley sugar, uh?"

"Yes, well, I sort of thought . . . " said Martin. "But Mr. Catch swore she'd never been in a smash."

"Correct," said Mr. Manayev. "And why? She never been more than fifty mile an hour is why. She belong to Harry Frome, little building-man up Scarrow Road, and he puts his own sidecar on her for carrying his ladders, uh? Is a good builder, but not for sidecars. How that frame is twisted!"

Jake grinned at the curious grunt by which Martin tried to suggest that this was what he'd suspected all along. Then Mr. Manayev looked over the moped, which was in very good nick as it was only a year since Granpa had given it to Martin and it had been kept in a garage and serviced by Martin with detailed love. Mr. Manayev got out a little book which listed dealers' prices for secondhand bikes of different makes and years and they settled on ninety-five pounds as a trade-in value for the moped.

"And two-twenty for the BMW?" said Martin.

"Two hundred," said Mr. Manayev.

"But you said — "

"Said is said. I was coming down to two hundred when you bargain with me. Your mother is still washing you behind the ears, uh?"

"Oh . . . thanks. What do you think, Jake?"

"OK by me."

"Right. It's a deal."

"Quick like that? What will you do for insurance?"

"I did the moped with my Dad's agent. We'll go back

into town and fix that, then I'll pick up a helmet for Jake and the cash for you. Back about three, with luck."

It took longer than that, so they didn't get home till nearly five. As he opened the door Martin heard it slither across paper on the mat, but the second post turned out to be only a letter for Mum. Nothing from Granpa. Perhaps the amusement and excitement of helping Martin buy the BMW made this seem more of a letdown than if Jake had simply come home from school and found nothing. At any rate it depressed him enough for Martin to look up half-way through tea and say, "What's up, Jake?"

"I wish Granpa would write."

"He's OK."

"I suppose so."

Silence. The flop of an oily page as Martin read his BMW maintenance manual. The far snore of a jet plane coming in to Eastleigh.

"Tell you what," said Martin suddenly. "Half term. Next week. I'd been thinking we might take the bike to Wales and I'd show you a bit of rock climbing. But if nothing's come from Granpa by then we'll ride up north and look for him."

2

ALMOST THE WHOLE of the journey from Southampton to Newcastle was dreary. For the first few miles Jake enjoyed the thrill of rushing air, the steady contented pulse of the engine, and the sense of making a start towards a place where he truly wanted to be. But the nag of the wind and the noise from the exhaust blotted out other feelings and sounds; the only variations came from the other traffic, being passed by a hurtling car on the right or passing a slow-moving lorry on the left; then for a few seconds there would be the drub of a different engine, the whine of tires and the buffet of displaced air. Even the smells were monotonous; it took something really pungent like a bonfire or a hardboard factory to penetrate the fuzz of exhaust and rubber and hot metal.

Five days earlier, when Martin had first ridden the BMW home from Mr. Manayev's, he had given Jake an earnest lecture on how important it was for the pillion passenger to keep his own body steady behind that of the rider, and not to try, when the bike leaned to take a curve, to lean the other way to right it. This lecture, Jake found, was quite unnecessary; because he couldn't see the tilting horizon, "down" for him was where he felt it to be. When the bike leaned for a corner, this sense of downwardness stayed in line with the bike, at the exact angle where gravity and centrifugal force canceled out. So Jake didn't even have the excitement which most pillion passengers enjoy in their first weeks of riding as they learn to master their instincts and trust the rider in front of them.

Holding himself against the soft warm leather of Martin's back, moving when his brother moved as if they were two branches of a tree which have grown almost into a single branch again, Jake passed the time by thinking about Granpa.

Most people in his life had begun as voices, or sometimes smells. Granpa had begun as a presence. Since he'd been a baby Jake had always woken early. One morning when he was five he had lain for a while listening to bird sounds and traffic sounds and decided that it would be a good hour before anyone else was up, so he'd slipped downstairs to the kitchen for a cup of milk. He'd taken his mug off its special hook and was opening the fridge when he'd realized that there was someone else in the room. Not Mum — she'd have started talking. Not Dad — there'd have been cigarette smoke. Martin never got up till he had to. No, there was a stranger sitting by the table, watching him.

He turned with the bottle in his hand and said, "Who are you? What are you doing in our house?"

"You're Jake," said a quiet, slow voice. Perhaps the man didn't want to wake the others, but it sounded as though he always spoke like that.

"Who are you?" said Jake.

"I'm your grandfather."

"No you aren't. Granpa's across the sea."

"They made me come home. They didn't give me time to write to your Mum."

Very vaguely, as if it had been part of his dreams, Jake remembered the tinkle of the door chimes and Mum's excited gabble.

"Oh," he said. "Well, hello, Granpa."

"Hello, Jake."

Jake felt for the mug he'd left on top of the fridge, poured it two-thirds full of milk, and put the bottle back. He could feel Granpa watching him all the time. He was proud of the way he did things for himself — several of his sighted friends weren't allowed to pour out their own milk because their Mums thought they'd spill — so he didn't mind showing off to Granpa.

"Shall I tell you a story about crocodiles?" asked Granpa suddenly.

"A true story?"

"I don't make things up, Jake."

"All right. I'll go and fetch my dressing gown."

When Jake came down again the kitchen was empty. He found his milk and went to the living room. It smelled of bedrooms, as if somebody had been sleeping on the sofa, but Granpa was standing over by the window, watching him again.

"You can sit down," said Jake. "But you mustn't put your feet on the chairs."

"I thought you couldn't see anything at all, Jake."

"Course I can't. And I won't ever, either. I don't mind."

"How did you know I was here?"

"I just knew. Did the crocodiles bite you?"

"They tried to. They bit a friend of mine very badly, so now he's only got one leg. You see, we were coming down this river . . ."

It was a good story, very exciting, a bit frightening and

all coming right in the end except for poor Toby's leg. But it wasn't at all like Dad's stories (though they could be exciting too, when they weren't just funny) because Jake knew all along that everything in it was absolutely true. When it was over Granpa asked a bit more about being blind, and about sometimes knowing things without being able to explain how, but by then Jake didn't mind because he knew that Granpa with his soft, slow voice was a friend, a real one, who he'd found for himself.

Now, looking back on it as he sat in a dreamlike stupor on the pillion of the BMW, Jake knew that all that first meeting had been exactly like Granpa — the gentleness and quietness and pleasure in amusing a small child, joined with the refusal to make a good story better by inventing extra bits and the patient insistence on trying to work out how Jake had known where he was, first in the kitchen, then in the living room. Granpa was nutty about explanations, especially explanations of mysteries. He would nag away at them until he was quite certain how a thing happened, or why it was there. Dad said this was what had got him thrown out of the African country where he'd spent all his working life as a mining engineer. As long as he'd stuck to showing how witch doctors did their tricks nobody had minded much; but then he'd started trying to find out why a whole pile of new machinery had turned up to be installed in a mine which was almost worked out, and he'd learned that somebody had paid somebody a colossal bribe for the order and one of those somebodies was married to the sister of the Minister of Something . . .

Dad said Granpa had been dead lucky, not just because his mining company had had to pay him quite a bit for being sacked so unfairly, but lucky to get out at all. If he'd nosed a bit further (Dad said) the odds were he'd have finished up dead at the bottom of one of his mine shafts, instead of being free to wander round Britain explaining away other people's ghosts.

That was what Dad said. You couldn't tell with Dad. He liked Granpa, but he liked a good story too, and he enjoyed the idea that nobody ever quite knew if he was telling the truth. Mum liked Granpa, of course, but she didn't understand him one bit. Jake found himself wondering whether Mum understood anybody — she didn't give herself much chance, always talking and never listening. Dad said her own mother had been just the same, which was why Granpa always spoke as if he didn't expect anyone to hear him, and why he'd gone to live in Africa too. Anyway, one of the things Mum couldn't understand was why Granpa refused to settle down in the cozy room she'd found for him a couple of streets away from the Bertolds, but spent eleven months of the year out with his camera and his tape recorder, trying to find explanations for well-known hauntings and wailings. Jake thought it was funny of Mum. It was so obvious. Granpa was like that, and you couldn't expect him to do anything else.

The engine quietened to a purr. The onrush of air slowed as the tires joggled over roughnesses. The bike tilted. When Jake reached his foot down he found unmoving rutted earth.

"Coffee stop. Sit on one of these things for more than a couple of hours and your arse becomes a lump of lead," said Martin. "Pretty boring for you I'm afraid, Jake."

"I'm all right. I've been thinking about Granpa and his ghosts."

"I've got a new idea about that. I hope we find the old boy because I want to see his face when I tell him."

The March air struck chill on Jake's scalp when he eased his helmet off. He slid his stick out of the scabbard arrangement Martin had made so that it could lie along the frame of the BMW, put the fingers of his left hand on Martin's forearm, and walked with him into the café.

While Martin fetched coffee Jake sat at a plastic-topped table and enjoyed the return of his senses — the muggy sweet smells of food, tobacco smoke and tea, and the rattle of cutlery and the clash and tinkle of the till and the wave-like wurra-wurra of voices. He tuned in to an argument among three men a few tables away.

". . . it's my livelihood, innit? Course I've got a right to say string the bleeding idiots up. I'd 'a done it meself, supposing I'd been there. Look, how long have I been driving? I'll tell you. Nineteen years, that's how long. I can remember when there wasn't no motorways. Could you do Southampton Carlisle in a day? You say yes, and I'll tell you you're a liar. So when a bunch of commie students gets it into their soft little heads to blow up motorways, I say bring back the death penalty and string 'em up."

"What I want to know," said a slower voice, "is why they go calling themselves Green bleeding Revolution-aries. Sounds sort of soft, uh?"

"Read about that, I did," said a younger voice. "There was this Green Revolution, it said. Summink to do with growing more rice in India and places. This lot of beggars just nicked the name."

"Talking of that," said the second man, "did you hear about Trevor? He was doing a run up to Hull with a load of babies' bottles when he had it nicked at that café north of Huntingdon. Bet the villains had a bit of a shock when they opened up Trevor's trailer and seen what they got! Eighteen thousand babies' bottles!"

"Nothing in 'em, I suppose?" said the first man. "No Scotch, I mean?"

Luckily they were still exploring this new problem when Martin came back. He was quite capable of getting into an argument with three lorry drivers about the merits of the GR movement. The coffee was baddish, but hot. Just in case Martin could hear as far as the lorry drivers, and just in case they came back to the death penalty for the motorway bombers, Jake said, "What's this new idea of yours?"

"I bet it isn't really new. Some SF writer must have thought of it. Ghosts don't come from the past, they come from the future."

"Then why are they sometimes dressed in wigs and ruffs and things?"

"The tourist agency got the machine setting wrong. There's this tourist agency in the future, running tours into the past, supplying authentic costume and that. They're exactly like any tourist agency, trying to do it on the cheap, so their machine keeps breaking down. That's why ghosts groan and howl and go about with their heads under their arms — it's just that parts have come through out of phase with other parts, and quite likely the agency has gone bust, too, and left them stranded here."

"I like it," said Jake. "But why are we afraid of them?"

"Um. Fear of the unknown?"

"Boring. Boring."

"What about this? It's not only tourists, it's baddies. People live forever in the future, and there's no death penalty, so the worst baddies get punished by being sent into the past. Not their bodies, just their inner selves . . ."

"Granpa won't go for inner selves."

"Silly old beezer. I've got an inner self and so's he. Anyway, the inner selves of these baddies hang around where their outer selves — their bodies — are in the future. They're like a bubble of wickedness waiting there, on a staircase, in a garden, in a wood. You go anywhere near, and you feel them. They infect you with fear."

Martin was very like Dad in some ways. Now he had lowered his voice to a tense whisper, almost as if he was trying to do what he'd described — build a little chill sphere of dread round them amid the noise and lively odors of the café. He paused, then his laugh at his own ingenuity pricked the fear bubble. Jake eased a biscuit out of its wrapping, taking his usual foolish care not to tear the cellophane, which he was going to throw away anyway. Crunching contentedly he fished in the breast pocket of his anorak for the pad of postcards Granpa had sent him, which he'd decided to bring in case they might help pick up the trail. They were all in order of sending, so he counted down to the tenth and ran his fingers over the row of pinpricks, neat as printed Braille, which Granpa used for writing to him.

"What about this?" he said, starting to read. " 'White Lady of Marsham. Wanders across churchyard and dives into tomb where inscription says occupant died for love.' "

"Funny sort of thing to have on your tombstone," said Martin.

" 'Ah, weep not! Though for love of Man I died,/Yet love of GOD shall raise me to His side.' "

"Uh-huh. What does Granpa say? Mist or something?"

"That's right. He got the vicar to have a bonfire five nights running, until the wind was right and the moon was right, and some of the puffs of smoke looked a bit like a woman drifting between the yew trees in a white wedding dress. It sounds OK to me."

"Maybe. But I think I could fit it in. Churches are funny — they go on staying in the same places even when the religion's completely changed. Whatever religion these people have in the future — "

"No use," said Jake.

Martin's chair scraped as he rose.

"What do you mean, no use?" he said. "I was just going to score a triple twenty."

"No use telling Granpa that," said Jake, picking up his stick and helmet. "If there's still a religion in the future he'll blow his top."

"What's he going to say to Saint Peter when he reaches the pearly gates? 'You're a figment of my imagination'?"

"Or, 'It's a trick of the light.' And he'll tell Peter about the mirages he saw in the Kalahari."

As Martin's laugh died Jake heard one of the lorry drivers saying, ". . . an what I say is, OK, you got to cover up a bit of country to build your roads, so you got less country to enjoy. But you gets it back, cause you gets quicker to the bits what's left, so you got more time to enjoy it, see?"

The boys spent that night near Derby at the home of a friend of Martin's called Terry McFadyen. Martin had come across Terry through the mysterious network of GR enthusiasts to which he now belonged. Jake hadn't realized how many of them there were. Despite this common interest the visit wasn't a success. To start with, Terry had forgotten to tell his mum that Martin had rung a couple of days before and asked if they could come. He'd just said, "Great. Great," and left it at that. He wasn't even in the house when the BMW drifted into silence at the curb and two very stiff-bottomed boys climbed off and knocked on the door. Mrs. McFadyen let them in but at once started telling them how inconsiderate Terry was, saying they could come without asking her; but when Martin started to say that they could easily go and find themselves a hotel room she wouldn't hear of it, and switched her fussing to Jake, trying to lead him round the house and settle him into chairs as though he were a helpless old cripple, and muttering about how far he was from home and what would his mother say if she knew. When Terry came home she switched back to him. She never stopped talking, just like Mum, but it wasn't like Mum's talk. Mum rattled on because she found everything so interesting or exciting or absurd (as though she were a radio commentator at the great procession of life, Dad said). Mrs. McFadyen talked in a heavy voice with a sigh or a tut in most sentences. There didn't seem to be a Mr. McFadyen, so Terry was all she had and all she thought about, and most of her thoughts were about making him different from what he was. For a short while she sighed and tutted at Jake, trying to talk him back to Southampton and talk Mum and Dad back from their lovely cornflake holiday. Then she tried to talk him into a home while they were away, as though he were some sort of pet dog which could be put into kennels. She cooked them a huge delicious supper, the beds were soft and warm, and breakfast was really good too, but it was a relief to say thank you and drown her sighing with the boom of the BMW's exhaust.

Halfway through the morning they had a nasty moment. Jake was leaning against Martin's back, vaguely wondering what life would have been like if Mum had been a fusser like Mrs. McFadyen, when the blare of a horn and the screech of tires pierced their own exhaust noise. Martin braked so hard that the deceleration shoved Jake against his brother's back. There was a lurch to the right and for one queasy instant down stopped being down. A fierce horn wailed close by, riding above the boom of a hard-driven big engine and the whimper of fat tires; then as the fast car pressed through on their right the buffet of wind it carried behind it seemed to straighten the BMW . . . and everything became as it had been before and they were humming up the road, steady and balanced. Only Jake could now feel through the leather a difference in Martin's body, a tension that relaxed in a series of spasms. Once or twice Martin spoke without turning his head, muttering his fright away.

They turned down a side road and picnicked by a canal. It was warm for March and Jake munched happily at a doughy roll and listened to the click and buzz of insect life and the occasional whip-plop of a fisherman's line fifty yards along the bank. Noon smelled of sluggish water and dank grass.

"Near thing this morning," said Martin suddenly.

"I was a bit scared. What happened?"

"Partly my fault — I was too close to the van in front of me, so I couldn't see when something pulled out in front of it. First I knew was the van braking like fury and skidding half across the road. I forgot you can lock the back wheel of the BMW if you brake too hard — that's the trouble with shaft-drive — so I got into a skid too. Even if we'd come off we'd have been all right — I was slowed right down by then — but we were almost out in the fast lane and there was this stupid great Jag coming through at ninety. Missed us by about six inches. Made me sweat a bit, I can tell you."

"Good thing Mrs. McFadyen wasn't watching."

Martin laughed.

"There was a police car after the Jag," he said. "I expect they took our number."

"Whatever for? You didn't do anything wrong, did you?"

"Witnesses or something."

"I'll say I didn't see anything and perhaps the bloke in the Jag will give me a fiver," said Jake.

Martin changed the subject. He still didn't really approve of Jake making jokes about his blindness.

"We'll be in Newcastle in a couple of hours," he said. "You sure Granpa didn't give you an address? Shall I look, in case he put it in ordinary writing?"

"Only the post office," said Jake, handing the wad of cards over.

"Stupid old beezer," said Martin as he flipped through them. "OK, we'll find ourselves beds first off. Any ideas about how we start looking for one rather loopy old pensioner in a city the size of Newcastle?"

This was absolutely typical of Martin. Jake had several times in the last few days tried to get him to think about it, but he'd refused to until the problem was staring him in the face. Jake had had to do his thinking on his own.

"Let me have my cards back. There was a list on the last one of things he was going to investigate. Here. Footsteps in a warehouse, a patch of cold air in a church, and a pub where the cat keeps getting into a shut fridge at night."

"No addresses?"

"No. He usually starts by looking up the local Psychic Society. We could ask them. And he goes to the local newspapers and looks at their ghost file."

"That's a start, I suppose. But the first thing is somewhere to sleep."

It didn't work out like that. An hour or so later Jake began to sense a change in the traffic flow, and a smokier smell in the air, and echoes off large buildings. A car drew level with the BMW, loitered for a while, then drew ahead. Martin stopped the bike and cut the engine.

"Cops," he muttered.

"Take it easy," said Jake.

Martin had nothing to prove it by, but he always spoke as though the police were out to frame him for some crime he hadn't committed. Now Jake could feel his tension as footsteps came towards them with that slow rhythm which means power and patience and apartness.

"Are you Mr. Bertold, sir?" said a voice that had the same weight and slowness as the steps.

"That's right," said Martin. "How —"

"Would you mind answering a few questions, sir? This lad is your brother?"

"Yes. We only —"

"Would you mind telling me what you are doing in Newcastle?"

"That's nothing to do with you. If you want to know about the accident —"

"What accident would that be, sir?"

There was no change of speed or emphasis in the dull voice, but beneath the surface Jake could sense a sudden throb of interest.

"There wasn't one," said Martin with a got-you-there tone. "There almost was, and we were almost in it, and I thought the police car that was chasing the Jag might have taken our number . . ."

"But he couldn't have taken our names, could he?" said Jake.

"They've got this computer —" said Martin.

"Now, wait a minute, sir," said the policeman. "This alleged accident what didn't occur is not the subject of our present inquiry. Would you be so good as to follow my car to the police station? We shan't detain you long."

"Now, look here —" said Martin.

"Let's go," said Jake. "It might be about Granpa."

"Oh, I suppose so," muttered Martin, obviously glad to get out of fighting a battle he wasn't going to win.

It was a longish ride, on wide roads at first, but then steeper and more crowded. They stopped in the stale openness of a car park, and went through swing doors into a place which smelled of linoleum and heated air and the peppery dust that goes with piles of paperwork. There were low voices and distant telephones and footsteps moving unhurriedly on known errands. The brothers waited for several minutes in a larger space where a very nervous man was explaining in a low voice about a wallet he'd found. He probably didn't realize that Jake could hear what he was saying. The man who was listening to him made notes, and between whiles tapped his pencil on a wooden counter, a noise as monotonous and impassive as a dripping tap.

A door opened. A man with a cold in his nose said, "Martin and Jacob Bertold? This way, please."

3

JAKE COULD HAVE followed the man's footsteps without help, but he kept his fingers on Martin's wrist because he was aware of the tension building up in his brother, a mixture of panic and anger which might suddenly make him do or say something really stupid. They went down a long corridor but before they'd reached the end the man stopped, knocked at a door, and opened it without waiting for an answer. Jake felt a pulse of surprise run through Martin's arm, followed by a sudden lessening of wariness.

"Come in," said a woman's voice. "Sit down. It's a bit cramped for three, I'm afraid. You're Martin and Jake Bertold? I'm Sergeant Abraham."

"Hello," said Jake, checking the position of the chair Martin had led him to.

"Hello," she said. "Please sit down, Martin. I'm sorry to bring you along here like this."

Jake began to build an idea of her in her tiny, office-smelling room. There were potted plants somewhere, recently watered. She wore quite strong-smelling scent and her voice was deep but not at all mannish. She knew she'd surprised Martin by not being a man and she thought that was funny. There was a vague suggestion of Mum about her, though she was shorter (or sitting on a very low chair) and a bit younger. She didn't have anything you could call an accent, but there was something a little careful about her vowels which suggested that she'd spoken differently when she'd been a kid and had taught herself to speak like this.

"What's up?" said Martin. The remains of resentment still hung round his voice like the leftover smells of supper which are sometimes lingering in the kitchen at breakfast.

"We got a phone call from a Mrs., er, McFadyen . . ."

"Oh!" said Martin, the last of his tension breaking into a laugh.

"Yes, well . . ." said Sergeant Abraham, half joining him. "Even so, I thought I'd better look into it. It came through to me because my job's helping kids sort out some of their problems — you know, runaways and that — so I asked the patrols on the Durham road to keep an eye out for you. It mightn't have worked, but it did. So now, though I think I know Mrs. McFadyen's type, I'd just like to satisfy myself that you *are* all right."

"I don't see —" said Martin.

"We're OK," interrupted Jake. "Our Mum and Dad are in the Bahamas. They won a three-week holiday off a cornflake packet. Martin's looking after me, but it's half term so we thought we'd come here and hunt for Granpa."

"Does your grandfather live here? Don't you know his address?"

"No. He travels around, but he sends me a postcard every week to say where he's got to. He hasn't written for three weeks and I don't know why. He's quite old. He's never missed before."

"And what is he doing in Newcastle?"

(She pronounced it Newcassel, with all the stress on the middle syllable.)

"Looking for ghosts," said Martin. Jake could hear he was hoping to get his revenge for her having startled him, but it didn't work.

"It takes all sorts," she said. "And the only way you know he's missing is that he hasn't sent a card for three weeks?"

"Well," said Martin. "We wanted to try out my new bike, too. There's that. But Jake was worrying himself stiff. I'd have given it another week, but this is half term, you see?"

"We had ours last week," she said. "Have you brought his last card with you, Jake?"

"You won't be able to read it, I'm afraid," said Jake, drawing the pack from his pocket and holding it out. "It's the one on the top."

"Braille?" she said. "Does he carry a machine with him, just to write to you? He's not blind too, is he?"

"No, of course not," said Jake. "He does it with a blunt pin. He taught himself. It's almost as neat as a machine, though."

"Heavens! That must take a bit of patience."

"He's like that," said Jake.

"He's a good guy," said Martin. "Nutty as a conker tree, but good with it."

"The postmarks are pretty regular," she said. "He doesn't say anything about not writing for a bit, does he?"

"No," said Jake. "Shall I read it to you?"

He reached out and waited for her to put the pack into his hand, then ran his fingertips over the pattern of tiny bumps.

"It's a bit like a telegram," he said. "He does it to save words. 'Newcastle. Fine town. Great be in mining country.

Friston Horror blank. No witnesses. Old map marks gibbet on spot. Now nosing alleged footsteps warehouse. Cold patch church. Pub where cats get into shut fridge. Expect plenty more big old dorp like this. If not heading north. Great walking country full bloody border murders. Tell parents have fun Bahamas. Rather them than me. Write GPO here.' "

"It sounds as if he expected to be here some time," said Sergeant Abraham. Jake thought he could hear a new undercurrent of seriousness in her voice, and she sat for several seconds in silence with her fingernail tapping the plastic of a telephone housing.

"Can you describe him to me?" she said.

She asked Martin very methodical questions, and made notes. Then she picked up the phone and dialed.

"Tom?" she said. "Poll here. I've got a missing person. Fairly definite. Ready? Right. John Uttery. Male. Five eight. Slim build. Sixty-three. Bald. Eyes brown. Small white mustache. Complexion tanned and mottled. Own teeth, good. Good condition. Khaki anorak, blue cord cap, brown polo-neck jersey, T-shirt, color not known, string vest. Gray slacks. Leather walking shoes, handmade. Educated voice. Military bearing. Left forearm severely scarred. Anything like that in the last three weeks? . . . Sure? . . . OK, check and ring me back, like a dove. Thanks."

The phone clicked.

"Well, that's a relief," she said. "He didn't go through the lists but he's pretty reliable. Nobody like your grandfather has turned up in any of the hospital accident centers or mortuaries. Not in the city of Newcastle, that is. We're putting out an automatic check through the neighboring districts. So where do we go from here? Do you know what your grandfather would have done when he got to a town like this? What sort of place would he have stayed in? Where would he have started looking for his ghosts?"

"He likes pubs," said Jake.

"That one where the cat got into the fridge?" she asked. "That sounds a bit screwy to me. Not really *ghosts*, is it? I wonder how he heard about it?"

"He'd have gone to the local newspaper and looked at the files," said Jake. "That's how he always started. And if there's a Psychical Research Society he'd have got in touch with them."

"We thought we'd start with the newspaper," said Martin, as though he'd planned it all out himself.

"You'll start by finding somewhere to sleep," she said. "I'll ring a couple of places for you, shall I?"

"That's awfully kind," said Martin, unable to keep the note of surprise out of his voice.

"No it isn't. I want you to keep in touch. You'll need to, anyway, in case we pick up a line on your grandfather. But I'm only protecting myself. Now that Mrs. McFadyen's rung me up I've got to keep a check on you, because if you *do* get into a mess I shall be in dead trouble."

"Honestly!" said Martin. "That woman!"

"I expect she thinks everybody's like Terry," said Jake.

Sergeant Abraham laughed as she picked up the phone.

She found them a room in a church hostel. The beds were hard but clean and dry, and the room itself snug. Jake was thankful for this as he lay awake and listened to the dwindling noises of the nighttime city. The racket of traffic was steadily being replaced by the rising wind, which had been sharpish from the northeast all day but now was hissing and grunting among the rooftops, and hooting where an edge of guttering caught it at a resonant angle. Was Granpa lying out somewhere, chilled and helpless under the nag and blunder of this rising storm? He wasn't in any of the hospitals, so Missing Persons said. Jake's own last letter was still uncollected at the post office. That was twelve days old. The one before had gone. At least that showed that Granpa had really vanished, and it wasn't just that his letters to Jake had been going astray. But it only made the situation clearer — it didn't make it any less worrying.

Of course it was wonderful to have the big police machine working to find Granpa, taking his disappearance as seriously as it took the thousands of other things it dealt with every day. Tomorrow that machine would be doing the routine search while Martin and Jake tried to check up on the ghosts Granpa had been interested in. Jake could see that they'd been extraordinarily lucky in having Mrs. McFadyen ring up and pester Sergeant Abraham about them . . . Yes, but what about Granpa?

He sighed and turned over. The shifting gusts of the storm echoed the pulses of worry in his mind. Martin had opened the window a crack, and as he drew breath for a second sigh Jake noticed something. The smell in the wind . . . All his life had been spent on the outskirts of a big port where, even among the traffic smells and the garden smells and the smells from local factories, there had always been a sort of undersmell, too faint and persistent to be noticed. Even when you went inland you weren't aware that it was missing. It was when you came back . . . and that's what he and Martin had now done. He could smell the sea.

But this was a different sea — not the busy, almost tamed English Channel, that High Street of Europe's shipping, but the wild, ship-foundering, man-drowning, gale-breeding North Sea. Only ten days ago, the night before Mum and Dad had left, Jake had listened to a TV documentary about oil rigs, and about how those gawky steel giants had to withstand the hill-high waves and merciless winds of the most dangerous water in the world. The journalist who had spoken the commentary had used that very phrase, and Martin had said "Hey! Come off it! What about Cape Horn?" and Dad had said that the most dangerous water in the world was the puddle that froze outside your back door, and Mum had said whose fault was that when Somebody insisted on washing his car there on frosty evenings . . . The most dangerous water in the world. It was curious that Jake found its nearness homely and comforting, but he did, and with the smell of salt in his nostrils he fell asleep.

The man who looked after the old files at the newspaper office was busy but friendly. He remembered Granpa.

"Pleasant old bird," he said. "Knew what he wanted, which is all that matters in this dump." *Brring*. "Drat that phone. Scuse me . . . Library . . . No, no, nothing on that, not one column inch. Not in my time . . . Course I'm sure . . . If you want to come and look for yourself you're welcome, but you'll be wasting your time . . . Bye." *Ting*. "Where were we? Yes, ghosts. File on that. Cold patch in Saint Fredegund's? Lot on that, all dead boring because it isn't there. Least, thermometers won't measure it. What I say is, tell people there's a horrible mysterious cold patch somewhere and shove 'em into it and naturally they'll shiver a bit, supposing they got any imagination at all." *Flip-flip-flip*. "There you are — that's your cold patch for what it's worth. Start by asking the verger — now, what's his name? Here. That's it — Hewison. Good Newcastle name, that. Used to be a greengrocer's — " *Brring*. "Scuse me. Library . . . Couple of minutes, Mac — I'll send 'em straight down." *Ting*. "Where were we? Cats in fridge — that's not on file. Collier's Arms, Barrow Way, tidy little pub. Told him that one myself. Footsteps in warehouse — only a couple of paragraphs on that, last November wasn't it?" *Flip-flip-flip.* "Thought so. That's all. Mice, I should think. Now, if you'll scuse me . . ."

Granpa had stayed at the Collier's Arms.

Mrs. Rankin, the landlord's wife, had a refined voice which slipped every now and then into a half twang. She sounded as if life were one long fret to her.

". . . Ooh, I do hope nothing's happened to him," she said. "Such a nice gentleman, and done us a real good turn. Didn't leave no address, except somewhere down Southampton way . . ."

"That's us," said Martin. "Our home, I mean. He didn't say where he was going?"

"Up north a bit, but he did say as he might be back, or he mightn't. I wasn't expecting him, exactly . . . Shall I show you the room he had? There's been no one in since."

They followed her up the narrow creaking stairs, but Granpa hadn't left anything behind, of course. The room didn't even smell of him. The three of them were hesitating in its musty silence when Martin said, "Did he have any luck with the cats?"

Mrs. Rankin drew her breath in sharply, then sighed.

"I suppose you've a right, sort of," she said. "But you won't tell anyone? He said not to tell anyone. It was our Tyrene. I still don't know how he got it out of her. We'd asked her, of course, but she's only three. She was jealous of the new baby, Mr. Uttery said — course, he does take up a lot of my time and I hadn't really noticed how I wasn't paying so much attention to little Tyrene — there's the pub to run and all, you see? Anyway, it seems when the baby was on the way I'd explained about it to Tyrene, and the way I'd done it was telling her about the time the cat had kittens, and poor little scrap she'd got muddled in her mind and she thought she could stop any more babies coming by shutting the cats away. Do you see? You probably can't remember how your own minds worked when you were that small."

Jake couldn't, but he remembered Granpa sitting in the lounge in the early morning telling a small boy a story about crocodiles.

"My husband wanted to wallop her," said Mrs. Rankin. "Two of the cats had died, you see. But Mr. Uttery talked him round and we took her to the circus instead, and I always give her a bit of a cuddle when she goes to bed and now far as I can see she's as happy as a lark. Oh! There's that dratted baby. I must run now. I do hope you find him, really I do."

"Mice!" growled Mr. Smith. "Mice *scuttle*, that's what A told him. Why yes, that's what A told him."

"But there's a sort which hop," said Jake. "If the space between the floorboards and the ceiling below is just right you get — "

"And that's what he told me!" interrupted Mr. Smith, making it sound as though he'd scored another point in the argument by being told the same thing twice.

They sat in his stuffy little front room. It smelled of dust and polish and coal. The chairs felt as though they weren't often used — prickly and slightly dank. Mrs. Smith, who had a creaking limp, had brought Mr. Smith's tea tray in from the kitchen and gone away without saying anything, but the tea had included a plate of smoked haddock whose lively pungency cheered the glum air of the place. Mr. Smith's voice had the same effect. He sounded elderly and spoke with a real Newcastle accent, a twanging lilt with most of the sentences rising up the scale as if they were trying to become questions. Jake had heard snatches of this talk in the streets and had barely understood a word because of its quickness and its strange, hard vowels, but Mr. Smith spoke it like an actor, as though everything he said was full of enormous interest which he wanted to share with his listeners. He was the security guard at the warehouse and had been sleeping most of the day.

"What happened?" asked Martin impatiently.

"Why, nothing," said Mr. Smith. "We sat up all night and not a footstep anywhere. Your granddad said it was mice and our voices frighted them away, but A told him it was a ghost and the same applied. A got him there, didn't A?"

"Are you sure it was Granpa?" said Jake. "His name's Mr. Uttery."

"Why yes. That's him."

"Only usually he doesn't let people even whisper while he's after one of his ghosts."

Mr. Smith cackled.

"There's silence enough in the warehouse other nights," he said. "A get sick of the sound of it. Why, yes, A got your granddad gossiping soon enough. It's only natural — a feller like him as doesn't believe in ghosts and a feller like me as does, we'd want to talk it over, wouldn't we? Talked all night, matter of fact. He knew a pile of good stories, spite of putting the wrong answers to most of 'em, and A told him two or three good ones back. A've got to keep my end up, haven't A?"

"What did you tell him?" asked Jake.

"Did you tell him any new ones?" said Martin at the same instant. Both boys almost yelled their question.

"Did A?" said Mr. Smith triumphantly. "You ought to

have seen him scribbling away in his little black notebook. Course, he knew already some of what A told him, but — "

"Could you tell us the ones he wrote down?" said Martin.

"Why yes," said Mr. Smith. "A'll lend you my pen, young feller, if you want to write 'em down too."

"No, it's all right," said Martin. "Jake'll remember."

Mr. Smith grunted, accepting the fact as if it were one of his ghosts, strange but true.

"Were they all in Newcastle?" asked Jake.

"Why no. But all up this bit of the world, if you follow me . . . A told him about the Bandon Curse for a start, but he knew that one. Amazing how thorough he'd been into it, reading all the books and that. Said it was a pile of coincidences and half of 'em hadn't happened either. Almost got *me* thinking there never was a curse at Bandon at all . . . Why yes, but he'd never heard of the Roman soldiers up on Sloughby. Sloughby Moor, that's getting along twenty miles north of old Hadrian's Wall. You get a lot of fogs up there, coming down sudden, catching hikers and such. Twice, far as A've heard tell, there's been a man up on Sloughby when a fog come, and he's lost the path and cast about to find it again. There's bogs up on Sloughby too, deep enough for a horse and cart to founder in but looking like good firm ground — so these fellers A'm telling you of, when they heard shouts in the fog they'd make towards them, running a bit when they get nearer, and all of a sudden they see the Romans, nine or ten of 'em, wearing skirts and brass armor, drawn up in a ring back to back and staggering around and slashing with their swords like they were fighting, when all the time there's nothing to fight but bits of mist. And then it comes on thick again, and the shouting stops, and when it clears there's not a Roman to be seen."

He was a good storyteller, quiet but dramatic. No wonder Granpa had decided to chat with him rather than listen for hopping mice.

"What do you think, Jake?" said Martin.

"It's his sort of thing, I suppose. At least it would be worth taking the bike up to Sloughby and asking the people who live round there —"

"Live round there!" exclaimed Mr. Smith. "Who's going to live up on Sloughby, saving it's a few grouse and ravens?"

"I think Granpa would go and look, anyway," said Jake. "What else did you tell him?"

"Why yes, A told him about Penbottle Pele. You lads know what a pele is, then?"

"Fraid not," said Martin. Jake could hear that he was interested and excited by the feeling that they were making progress in their hunt, but at the same time irritated by having to listen to a lot of stories about ghosts and longing to get on the BMW and roar up to the moors.

"A pele's sort of halfway between a house and a fort," said Mr. Smith. "For years and years those murdering Scotties would come raiding down across the border, burning what'd burn and stealing what'd steal. You're a farmer, miles out from any walled town, so what do you do? You build your house like a fort, stone walls a yard thick, doors of four-inch oak, not a window less than twelve foot from the ground and those no bigger than a man can poke his head through. You have just the one big room downstairs and that's your cattle barn or byre, and you have steep little steps, like a ladder almost, running up the outside of the house to the rooms above where you live. So when the reivers come raiding you can shut your cows in the barn and your family and yourself in the upstairs. And the Scotties take a look at your pele and go off to find a softer nut to crack, or failing that they get into your barn and drive your cows away, but they leave you and your kids unmurdered, not being worth the trouble. That's a pele."

"Did it always work?" asked Martin.

"Why no. Maybe the Scotties would starve you out, or maybe they'd burn you out, but that's not what happened at Penbottle. The pele there belonged to a rich farmer, a sort of cousin of Lord Percy, A've heard it said, and he'd built it like a castle. One night when the Scotties came they battered at his door till morning without getting in while he mocked 'em from above. And the dawn came, and they started to skulk away, and the farmer took his crossbow and shot at the last man and nailed him, and that man was first son of the chief of the Scotties. And when the second son saw his brother was dead he cried out a vengeance on the farmer, and the farmer laughed. But for all his mockery and laughter he was a careful man so he sent word of what had happened to his cousin Lord Percy, and next time the Scotties came he let 'em get into the barn, but it was full of Lord Percy's soldiers and they killed almost every man of the Scotties, the chief's second son among them. Now that chief had three sons, and the last of 'em had gone to soldier for the King of France. But when he heard of how his brothers had died he came traveling back through England, making out he was a Frenchie and peddling bits of silk and pretty trash. So in course of time he came to Penbottle Pele asking for shelter. A've forgotten to tell you this farmer had a wife . . . why, don't they say there's more ways through a door than kicking it down? That third brother, he must have been a handsome lad, and known it. The farmer gave him supper, and by way of thanks he sang French songs at the hearthside, and gave the wife a fine silk scarf from Paris, and went his way in the morning . . . So there . . . Course, there were days when the farmer would have to travel to town, or to his cousin Lord Percy's castle, and he'd come late home, and one such night he rode up the path and saw the lantern shining in his little window and the smoke going up from his chimney, silver in the moon . . . You go to Penbottle Pele on a night like that, young fellers, and maybe you'll see . . ."

Mr. Smith stopped and coughed a little embarrassed cough.

"It's all right," said Jake. "I know what you mean. Go on. What'd I see, supposing I could?"

"Sorry, laddie, A got carried away. There's no roof to Penbottle Pele now, and no floors neither, only the four thick walls and the little stair leading up to the narrow doorway. But on a moonlit night a man who climbed the stair and looked through the door might see a woman opposite him. He might think she was standing, or maybe dancing, though there's no floor to stand or dance on; and then he'd see that she wasn't either, but she was hanging, not that there's a beam to hang from. And he'd know that he was seeing just what that farmer saw before the Scotties cut him down, his own wife that had betrayed him hanging from the roof beam in front of his own hearth."

There was a longish pause before Martin said, "Nasty," and Jake said, "What did Granpa think?"

"Questions, questions," grumbled Mr. Smith. "You're as bad as he was. How did A learn the story? My granny told me. How'd my granny learn it? Her granny told her."

"Granpa says you hardly ever find somebody who's actually seen a ghost," said Jake. "They always know somebody else who saw it, only that somebody's dead or something."

"Obstinate old feller," said Mr. Smith. "That's what he said when A told him about Annerton Dike Mine. Coming from the south you won't have heard of the Annerton Dike Disaster.''

"Can't say I have," said Martin.

"Why yes," said Mr. Smith. "Annerton Dike Disaster, 1837, and your granddad expects me to find someone still alive for him that was there!''

"Is that a ghost too?" asked Jake.

"Why no. Not a ghost exactly. Can't say A know what it was. My granny told me again, and that's as good as you'll get because her uncle Jack was the only one, man, woman or boy, to come out of the mine alive that day. Annerton Dike, up beyond Alnwick. A don't know if you've heard, but there's no good natural harbors between the Tyne and the Tweed, so to fetch their coal away the coalmasters had to *make* harbors. Why yes, even Blyth, that's a made harbor. Annerton Dike was a middling pit for those days. There was about a hundred men and women working it, right on the coast, with its own little harbor. There'd always been mining there, since Domesday. Why yes, Annerton's in Domesday. Think of that! But at first they'd only drifted in from the cliff . . .''

"Drifted?" said Martin. "Doesn't sound very strenuous.''

"That means the coal seam came out at the surface and they were able to get at it sidelong," said Mr. Smith. "But coal seams don't lie level, and at Annerton the seam ran tiltways up into the hill, so when the big iron founders and steel founders started and they was begging for good coking coal, it paid the coalmaster at Annerton to sink a pit from the top and fetch the coal out that way. That's the main Annerton Pit, where the disaster was.''

"What happened?" said Martin.

"Why, nobody knows.''

"I thought your granny's uncle got out alive."

"A'm coming to that," said Mr. Smith mysteriously. "Those days, when a miner died in a pit, there was never an inquest. Think on that! What's a few dead miners, they said, when there's coal to be won so as the coalmaster's missus can buy a few more diamonds to wear at the balls in London? So there was never an inquest at Annerton, though there was questions in Parliament and a bit of a fuss in the London papers. But the papers up here, they belonged to the coalmasters too. A whole shift dead, forty-seven men and women and boys and girls — why yes, they'd little girls in the pits them days, younger than you are, laddie — and the papers said it was from natural causes! Eeya! Think on that!"

Metal and china clattered as he slid his plate across the table. Then the little room filled with the reek of treacle-sweet tobacco. Jake heard the faint whisper of paper being carefully rolled into a cigarette.

"Where's the ghost?" said Martin.

Mr. Smith grunted, too absorbed in getting his smoke just as he wanted it to think of anything else. At last he lit up.

"Why yes, the ghost," he said. "Now there's one thing you've got to know about Annerton. They had never any trouble with gas, never any explosions or foul air. Don't ask me why — there's pits like that, and there's others where you're in trouble if the fans stop for a couple of hours only. Now there's a tip at Annerton on the cliff top — not a tall pointy one like you see from the railways, more of a big mound. You know what a tip is? Why, it's everything that comes out of a mine that they can't sell as coal. They'd have dumped it in the sea, except that they didn't want to go silting up their harbor. So there's this thundering weight of rock and stuff on top of the cliff that God

❖ 48

never set there. Maybe it was that, maybe it was something else, but all of a sudden, July nineteenth, eighteen hundred and thirty-seven, the men working above ground heard the whole hill groan. Like a great beast in pain, it was. And then there came a crash and next thing they knew was the main shaft had all caved in. It was lined with timber, of course, but my granny told me it was just as though the hill had clutched that timber like a man crumpling a letter in his fist. And there was forty-seven miners trapped below!"

"How far down?" said Martin.

"Not far. Why no, twenty fathom, something like that. Course, the night shift was back at the pithead straightaway, and digging. They was full of hope, because like I told you Annerton was always a clean pit. So they dug all the first day, until toward evening somebody come from the shore saying they'd found my granny's uncle Jack wandering down there, clean out of his wits. My granny wasn't born then, of course, and Jack was only a boy. He was drenched with water — not seawater — and they made out he must somehow've got himself washed out down the drainage cut that carried the water out of the pit. They got no answers out of him, so his Mum put him to bed and he lay there, shuddering and weeping until the pneumonia caught him and he near died of that. Course, there was no way back along the drainage cut, but his getting out so unexpected made them look for other ways in, and while the digging went on at the main shaft they thought to explore down an old by-pit. A by-pit's more of a ventilation shaft, but sometimes it'll have rungs in it, or an iron ladder, if the pit's not a deep one. So there was this by-pit, and that was blocked too, but nothing like so bad, and they'd dug their way down through it by the middle of next morning. And what did they find?"

"You tell us," said Martin.

"Why, yes, A will. They found the rock slip had not been down in the mine at all. It was in the layers of rock above, and the coal seam was just as it always was, with only a bit of a roof fall here and there. And the air was good and clean too. But every miner, man, woman and child, was dead. Dead and cold. And the face men that should have been trying to dig them out from below had dropped their picks in the galleries, and they'd all clustered to the foot of the shaft, and there they'd died. Not starved, not gassed, not burned. Just died."

"What of?" asked Martin.

"Ask your granddad," said Mr. Smith sharply. "A'm telling you what A *know*. They brought the bodies up through the by-pit, and never a man of them would go down into Annerton Mine again. There was still coal down there, but the coalmaster couldn't hire the miners to work it. The word went around that there was something in Annerton Pit, or maybe just that it was an unlucky pit —"

"What do you mean, something?" said Martin.

"A don't know. But my granny's uncle Jack, he lived a long while and he never got his wits back. Not that he was raving mad. They never needed to put him away. But he couldn't speak sense, and some days he'd sit from morning to night in the corner, shuddering. Only when he came to be dying and my granny was sitting by his bed he woke up in the middle of the night and looked at her like he'd suddenly remembered who he was. 'We let it out,' he said. 'We loosed it from the rock.' He said it quite plain, though for forty years he'd never done more than mumble. And then, before she could ask him what he was talking about, he was dead."

THE BMW GROWLED up the slope as though it were gnawing its way to the top of Sloughby Moor, bouncing and bobbling on the rough track, but when Martin cut the engine the huge peace closed round Jake like a dream of space and silence. It was as though the noise of the bike had been a pain, a wound, which the quietness flowed in to heal.

"Can't take her any farther," said Martin. "We'll have to walk if we want to go on. What a place! I wouldn't mind tramping fifty miles, and I bet I'd never see a soul."

Jake lifted his helmet off and let the wind ruffle through his hair. The silence wasn't dead, or absolute. A curlew called and was answered some distance away, and farther still a tractor engine toiled, but distance dwindled the sound of it to a whispering tock. All the while the bitter wind hissed through grass stems, a wind empty of smells, air as clean as water.

"What's it look like?" said Jake. It wasn't a question he often asked.

"Bare," said Martin. "I can't see a house or a tree. That

next hill's got stone walls running up it, straight as a ruler. If we go along the path here we'll come to heather pretty soon. It'd be easy to get lost, even without fog coming down, because the hills flow into each other. No landmarks. I don't mean it's shapeless. It's like the flank of a horse, fawn colored, with heather-colored blotches, and we're a couple of ants or something. Feel like a walk, ant?"

"OK."

The path was only wide enough for one, so Martin picked his way through the tussocks beside it with Jake's fingertips on his wrist. They walked nearly half a mile and stopped again.

"Well?" said Martin.

Jake stood still, trying to shut the present out of his mind, trying not to hear the hiss of the wind or feel its chill nagging. He concentrated on the moor, which had been here always. He knew he could usually tell when Granpa was in the same room with him, so perhaps now he might be able to sense faint traces of his having walked along this path a week ago. But he felt nothing.

"I don't know," he said. "I'm not a bloodhound, Mart."

"No need to get shirty," said Martin. "It was worth a try. Anyway, I'm glad to have come, for its own sake."

"How'd Granpa have got up here, anyway?"

"There's bus stops on the bottom road. That's about four miles off."

(Granpa could have afforded a small car but he preferred the company he found on buses and trains. Sometimes he hired a taxi to visit a really isolated ghost; Sergeant Abraham was getting someone to ring round the Newcastle taxi firms and check, though Jake doubted whether he'd have thought it worth it for Roman soldiers only seen by hikers in fog.)

"I expect Sergeant Abraham could ask the bus company," said Jake.

"Right. And if we go back the other way we can stop at — what's it called? — Burlaw and ask at the pub if they've seen a loopy old ghost hunter saying which way to the Romans. He's bound to have come one of those ways."

"He'd probably do that himself — go one way and come back the other, I mean — so he could ask at pubs and post offices. That's what he usually does."

"OK, that'll rule out Sloughby. Let's get back to the bike and out of this wind. I want my lunch."

Penbottle Pele stood nearly a mile out of Penbottle village, along a farm track. The woman at the pub had told them to ask Mr. Yerby about the ghost, and he'd turned out to be an ancient cottager who had elected himself as the local expert on the subject. He told them the same story as Mr. Smith, but not half as well. A few details were different, such as the wife not being hanged by the Scots but hanging herself after her husband's death. He hadn't seen Granpa, which almost proved Granpa hadn't been there, but they rode down to the pele nonetheless.

It was a heavy, oppressive place, smelling of cow dung and rotting grass. When Jake stood in the middle of the space where the byre had been (and which was still used by cattle sheltering from the wind) he could sense the rough and massive walls reaching up towards the square of sky at the top. They seemed to be leaning inward, as if they were still clutching in a miser's grasp the rooms that had once lain between them. The rank air at ground level was still, but higher up leaves shuffled gently where shrubs had found roothold in the tower walls. Leather scraped on stone fifteen feet up.

"She's not there now," said Martin's voice. "Far as I can see, that is. There's the hole where the beam ran, and there's the hearth. The windows are incredibly small. It must have been a pretty dismal place even when it had a roof and things."

"It feels dismal now."

"You've been listening to too many ghost stories."

That might be true, thought Jake. Granpa often said that if you told people that a place was frightening, or that something frightening had once happened there, they'd be more likely to feel frightened when they went. You didn't have to believe in a ghost still dangling in the moonlight from a beam which had rotted centuries ago; the story itself was enough to produce a shudder, as though time were a wire which still vibrated to the touch of that particular cruelty. Jake used his stick to find a path between the cowpats and reached the door in time to hear Martin coming down the steep outer stair.

"Well?" said Martin again.

"I don't know," said Jake. It was too difficult to explain. Suppose it had been possible to do the bloodhound trick, to pick up, somehow, traces of Granpa's personality after he'd left, then the moor had been too empty and bare and the pele was too crowded and muddled. It would be like trying to pick out a single whisper across a playground of yelling kids. And it probably wasn't possible anyway.

"OK," said Martin. "Don't let's worry. He'd be bound to have talked to Mr. Yerby. So that's two off the list for Sergeant Abraham. I suppose it's progress of a sort."

It was more than an hour's ride to Annerton Dike. Last night's gale had blown itself out but seemed to have left patches of cleaner, colder, saltier air inland; after a while, though, Jake was sure they were traveling with the sea itself only a mile or two away to their left. They passed through a small town and spun along a good main road for quarter of an hour. Then the bike slowed and turned seaward. Now the road was a quiet lane which twisted sharply several times, usually at right angles, as though it were running through a village; but from the echoes of the exhaust Jake could hear that there were no houses anywhere near, only low banks or ragged walls on either side, and nothing much beyond them. Then the road straightened again, but after a couple of minutes Martin stopped the bike and throttled back. Now Jake could hear the sea and smell the sting of salt.

"No entry. Road closed. Danger falling rocks," called Martin through the burring engine noise. "There was a sign at the main road saying the hotel and the caravan park wouldn't be open till May. Hell!"

"Where are we?"

"Top of a cliff. There's a sort of harbor place down at the bottom. Quite a big yacht there, and what looks like a pub. Caravan site. The road's a real slope — it looks dangerous enough without the falling rocks — Hey! Something's been down there since last night's rain! Truck of some sort."

"What's that over there?" said Jake, waving to his right where there seemed to be a sort of gap in the wide march of the wind off the North Sea.

"Must be the old mine tip, I suppose," said Martin. "Looks like a ruddy great burial mound. Good place for a picnic on a fine day — you could see miles — it's right on top of the cliff. That must be what caused the disaster."

"I expect so. Listen, Mart — Granpa never pays attention to 'No Trespassing' notices and things like that. I think seeing we've come so far —"

"So do I. Hold tight."

Martin revved the engine and took the bike slowly forward. The tilt was as sudden as that of a slide in a children's playground — Jake used to love going down the slide when he'd been small. Martin picked a path over a slithering, rutted surface. The engine coughed and popped and its echoes coughed and popped back off the cliff to their left. The salty updraft from the waves came in sudden gusts. Then the track leveled and its roughness changed to the wincing regularity of cobbles. There was a smell of mutton stew in the air, penetrating the stinging sharpness of the sea and mixed with the faint but unchanging odor of pubs, stale beer and oak and vinegar. Martin cut the engine. Jake eased himself off the pillion, loosened his helmet, and slid his stick out of its sheath. He heard the sea wind gusting against the flat front of a building on his left. A curtain flapped in an open window. Over to the right a wire halyard clinked irritably against the metal mast of a yacht. A gull mewed by.

"Pretty in a bleak sort of way," said Martin. "Very pretty on a sunny day, I should think, though those caravans are an eyesore. Time somebody invented a burrowing caravan, so that everybody could go and camp in beauty spots without spoiling them for everybody else. Otherwise there's only this pub and some beat-up buildings the other side of the creek — something to do with the old mine, by the look of them."

"I can smell cooking," said Jake.

"So can I. A hotel, but it looks pretty shut. Hang on."

He strode away. Jake heard a light rattle and thud as he tried the door.

"Locked," he called. "I'll try round the back. You be all right?"

"Fine."

Martin's footsteps and the squeak and brush of his leathers vanished round a corner. Jake leaned against the bike, enjoying the slight updraft of warmth that rose from its cylinders. Good old bike, he thought. I hope Dad understands . . . there's going to be another gale tonight — the sea sounds hungry. Now, where am I?

Close by, Jake could hear the lap and slosh of smallish waves breaking against a regular surface — the seawall, presumably, but protected from the larger, noisier waves by some sort of mole further out. There was a steady, even growl running across a fair arc of sea to windward, and then somehow becoming more irregular to left and right as it dwindled away. Jake cocked his head this way and that, picking out separate pieces of the general roar, until he was pretty certain that he was standing on a quay at the narrow end of a funnel-shaped inlet — a broad, flat funnel — formed by the dike running into the sea. The harbor mole cut off a triangle of calmer water this end. Over to the right as he faced out to sea were cliffs, not very high, with the mound of the tip on top of them. That was where the mine had been. To the left the land seemed to slope down less ruggedly — at least there seemed to be nothing that side to toss back scraps of echoes — so perhaps that was where the caravans stood empty, waiting for another tide of summer visitors. Just before Martin's footsteps came back he picked out a rhythmic clank from below the cliffs to the right. It didn't sound the kind of noise the wind could set up.

"Not much help," said Martin. "Only a batty old girl peeling spuds. Pub only becomes a hotel summer weekends and holidays — otherwise the landlord opens as he feels like. He's got a gang of friends here, industrial archaeologists by the sound of it, studying the old mine.

She said she hadn't seen Granpa. But she didn't sound as if she'd really know whether she'd seen him or not."

"There's somebody working over that side. I heard hammering."

"That'll be the archaeologists. Let's go and try there. Just the sort of thing Granpa would poke his nose into."

"He said in his card it was great to be in mining country."

"Right. Leave the bike here, I should think."

They walked back over the cobbles. From habit Jake registered directions and distances, though he wasn't likely ever to come here again. Nine paces beyond the point where the hotel front ceased to catch the wind, letting it rush on to buffet the main cliff, Martin led off a little to the left along a rough track squelchy with mud and sea slime. The rumble and grunt of the larger waves against the mole came nearer.

"Could have got the bike along here," said Martin. "Somebody else has been — Landrover by the look of it. And they've been putting shingle down on the dicey bits . . . Here's somebody."

A heel gritted on gravel. Then there was the dullish plop of a rubber sole on planking.

"Afternoon," said Martin.

"Good afternoon. Didn't you read the notices?"

A man's voice, something like a teacher's, slightly too clear and precise but with a touch of a slurrier accent beneath the surface.

"Yes, but this is important," said Martin. "We're looking for our grandfather. His name's Mr. Uttery."

"Sorry, can't help you."

"You might have seen him, though. There's a good chance he came here about ten days ago or a bit more."

"What's he look like?"

"Oh . . . thin and small, but not bent. Bald. He'd be wearing a blue corduroy cap and a khaki anorak and gray flannel trousers. He's got a little white mustache and a brown face, rather wrinkled."

"Can't say I've seen anyone like that."

The words were polite, but Jake thought it didn't sound as if the man had even thought about it.

"Perhaps somebody else has," said Martin.

"Who else?"

"Isn't there a party of students doing research into the mine?"

"Yeah. I'm one. But we're pretty busy — trying to cram a lot of research into a ruddy short time. What makes you think he might have been here? It's right out of season."

"Well, he's gone missing," said Martin, "and —"

"Been to the police?" said the man.

"Yes. They're doing the routine kind of search in Newcastle —"

"Then what are you up to, looking thirty miles north?"

The man sounded more impatient than ever, but somehow also interested.

"Granpa's a ghost hunter, you see," said Martin, and paused for the usual query or grunt of surprise. He didn't get it.

"No ghosts here," said the man as casually as if he'd been denying that he knew the time. This seemed to irritate Martin.

"You've heard of the Annerton Dike Disaster?" he asked.

"Can't say I have. This is Annerton Dike all right, though."

"The point is Granpa met an old man in Newcastle who

told him about a ghost here, something to do with the disaster, as well as ghosts at Penbottle and up on Sloughby Moor. We think he might have come to look."

"Listen, I'm not interested in ghosts. I haven't time for that kind of rubbish."

"But Granpa is, and we're looking for him."

"Well, try those other two places. He hasn't been here."

"We've done that. No dice."

"There you are then."

"Look," said Martin, "we've got to ask around. It won't be much use going back to Newcastle and telling the police we only talked to one of you. They'd only have to send a man out specially to ask the rest."

The man let out a long, impatient breath.

"Oh, all right," he said. "You'll have to stay this side of the bridge. The buildings are in a dangerous condition, and we aren't insured for anyone except ourselves."

"Thanks," said Martin. Jake relaxed slightly. While he'd been arguing Martin's voice had become steadily slower and deeper, a sure sign that he felt he was being pushed around and was trying to keep a hold on his temper. Although he'd won his argument, this wasn't the moment to go putting fresh suspicions into his mind. A mutter of voices gusted on the wind — presumably the man was asking his friends whether they'd seen Granpa, though the rhythm of the phrases was more like a discussion or argument. One of the voices was a woman's. After several minutes footsteps sounded again on the planks. This man was heavier, walked with longer strides and wore leather shoes.

"I hear you're looking for your grandfather," said a warm, deep voice.

"That's right," said Martin.

"Sorry to say we can't help you. Must be quite a worry

for you. I've checked with all the students, too. I think one of us would have been bound to see him if he'd come this way during daylight."

"He'd have come poking around anyway," said Martin. "He used to be a mining engineer."

"Did he now? Then they'd have welcomed him with open arms. Look, let's go back to the pub and I'll rustle up a cup of tea and take down a few details. Then we'll know who to get in touch with supposing your grandfather does turn up. My name's Jack Andrews. I'm the landlord at the pub."

"Oh. Fine," said Martin. "We're Martin and Jake Bertold."

"Very plucky of you coming all this way to look for the old man," said Mr. Andrews. Jake could tell from the slight extra heartiness that he was talking about Jake being blind.

"How did you know we'd come a long way?" said Martin.

"Southern accent," said Mr. Andrews with a laugh. "Sticks out like a sore thumb. I make a hobby of guessing where my customers come from during the season. Let's think. You'll be somewhere south of London, a bit west but not too far."

"Bang on," said Martin. "Southampton."

Mr. Andrews laughed again.

"Police been much help to you?" he said.

"Not bad," said Martin. "They took us seriously, which was more than I thought they'd do. They're checking the hospitals and things, but they let us go and do the ghosts. I suppose that was a bit much to expect of them."

"I must say I'd never heard of a ghost here," said Mr. Andrews. "Don't go spreading it about, or it might be bad for business."

"I don't think it's in the hotel," said Martin. "It's supposed to be in the mine. You've heard of the Annerton Dike Disaster?"

"Heard of the only bit of history that ever happened in this dump? Course I have. What about it?"

By the time Martin had finished telling the story they had reached the hotel and Mr. Andrews had led them through a side entrance into one of those stuffy-smelling rooms which you find only in rather crummy hotels, full of a mixed odor of dog and dust and stale tobacco ash. Jake settled into a large armchair upholstered in slippery leather.

"Not much to go on," said Mr. Andrews with one of his laughs. "Right, tea. May be a bit of time. Depends how hot the kettle is."

The door opened and shut.

"Funny setup," said Martin in a low voice.

"Yes," said Jake.

"You really think so?" said Martin, suddenly tense as a drumskin.

"Granpa's been here. They've seen him."

"Sure?"

"About usual."

Jake hadn't meant to say this until they were well away from Annerton. It was so difficult to know how Martin would react. In fact Martin gave a long, shuddering sigh.

"Listen," he said. "That first bloke hadn't heard of the Annerton Dike Disaster, and he's supposed to be studying the history of this mine. And we weren't getting anywhere with him till we said it'd mean a policeman coming out here . . ."

"And they both asked about the police," said Jake.

"Right. And Mr. Andrews knew where we'd come from. And where did that first bloke go?"

"What do you mean?"

"When he met us he was going somewhere, or at least pretending to. But when he'd gone back to the big shed he didn't come out again. I think he was a sort of sentry — Look, Jake, we don't *know* anything, not even you!"

Jake frowned and put his finger to his lips.

"OK," said Martin in a lower voice. "We won't say anything here. We'll go and tell Sergeant Abraham, soon as we get back to Newcastle."

Jake heard a slither and the flutter of paper as Martin picked up a magazine and did his usual fidgety leafing to and fro. Mr. Andrews's footsteps sounded at last in the passage. There was a clink of cups as the door opened.

"Sorry to be so long," he said. "Suddenly remembered I had to make a phone call. Now, milk and sugar both of you? Good. Keep the cold out. You wouldn't care to put up here for the night, would you? The wind's getting up, and it's going to be a nasty ride back to Newcastle."

"I thought you were full up with the students," said Martin.

"Oh, a couple of them can double up."

"Oh . . . very kind of you . . . what do you think, Jake?"

"I think we'd better get back to Newcastle," said Jake slowly. "We don't want Sergeant Abraham to have to look for us too."

"It's very kind of you, sir —" began Martin.

"Jack," said Mr. Andrews. "Sir is a dirty word round here. OK, let's get a few details down. Your grandfather's name is . . ."

He took quite a bit of trouble, but the only new oddity was his little snort of laughter when he discovered that Sergeant Abraham was a woman. He asked several questions about her, and what her exact powers and responsibilities were. He also wanted to know how the boys had heard about the ghost, but made it sound like simple curiosity. Martin had left Mr. Smith's address behind, and Jake decided not to remember it. The tension grew steadily tauter, until Jake almost dropped his cup when he heard a board creak behind him to his right when he was quite certain there was no one there but the three of them. Oh, yes, there must be a connecting door to the next room. There was someone close to it — more than one person . . . Mr. Andrews put his pen down with a snap.

"OK," he said in a slightly louder voice. "Let's go."

As Jake stood up, two doors swooshed open and several people rushed into the room. Martin shouted. Crockery rattled to the floor. Amid the thuds Martin's next shout was muffled into a gulp.

"Stop it," said Mr. Andrews. "We're not going to hurt you."

For the few seconds it lasted Jake stood perfectly still. His heart was hammering and he longed to yell, but he'd long ago learned that in playground rough-and-tumbles he was less likely to get hurt if he wasn't moving. The sound of struggle stilled into panting.

"Jake's got the right ideas," said Mr. Andrews. "Now, listen, you two. We can't let you go for reasons of our own. We'll have to keep you here for a bit. But I promise you that if you do what you're told you won't get hurt. Right, Dave and Jeannie take Jake up to the park. I want to talk to Martin."

"Mart, are you all right?" said Jake.

There was a grunt which might have meant anything.

"Let him speak," said Mr. Andrews.

"You bastards. You bastards," said Martin. His sobs were fury and not pain.

"This way," said a woman. She sounded as though she was speaking through cloth. Cold, firm little fingers took Jake by the wrist.

"Now, look here . . ." shouted Martin.

"I'll be all right, Mart," said Jake in a shaky voice.

As he allowed the woman to lead him through the door he heard another thud and a grunt. Somebody stood on a cup. The woman who was guiding him made a little clicking noise with her tongue like a teacher disapproving of a naughty infant.

She led him out by the way they had come in, and then round and along the front of the hotel. Automatically Jake counted the paces — twenty-three to the edge of the cobbles, sixty-two along a track graveled in places with tinkling ash, twelve down a steep slope rutted with car tracks, nine across a wooden bridge.

On the far side of the bridge the path sloped steeply up slithery grass, not used enough to be trodden to bare earth. The sea wind hissed among short tussocks on either side, but its movement was muddled by large, solid shapes, too regular and resonant to be rocks. A taut rope whined. The path twisted. They were moving though the caravan park which Martin had mentioned. After eighty-seven paces the woman stopped. The man, Dave, who hadn't spoken a word but had walked steadily behind, brushed past. Jake heard, low down and a few feet in front of him, the clank of metal and then a steady, grinding rumble. When it stopped the woman said, "Stand still," and left Jake. A key clicked, a padlock rattled, hinges squeaked.

"This way," said the woman. "Two steps. There. Forward and turn left."

Jake climbed the metal steps into a narrow passage, smelling of plastic, rubber-backed carpet, dust, stale bread, butane, a chemical toilet — yes, a caravan. There was another presence there, familiar and comforting as the hallway at home after a wet tramp up from the bus stop.

"You've got a visitor, Mr. Uttery," said the woman in a bleak, ironic voice.

5

"ELLO, GRANDPA," said Jake. His voice was a shivering gasp. Since they'd taken him away from Martin he'd managed to control himself, to think, to count paces, to act deliberately passive and feeble. But now he wasn't on his own anymore he almost gave in to the wave of fear-sickness that seemed to rush at him out of nowhere.

"Jake!" said Granpa. "Why are you here? Are you all right? Have they hurt you?"

"No. I think they hit Martin, though."

"Thumped him a bit," said the woman in her oddly muffled voice. "No serious damage. Do you want to go to the toilet, Mr. Uttery?"

"Yes, please."

"Dave's outside, so don't do anything stupid."

Jake found himself firmly twisted and pushed onto a padded bench, as though the woman were playing with a large doll. Again a chain rattled and a key clicked. Blankets flopped and Granpa got to his feet with a slight groan. He seemed to Jake to come very shakily down the caravan towards the chemical toilet, but he didn't say anything. On his way back he reached out and patted Jake's shoulder, his hand brushing past Jake's cheek as he withdrew it. It was as cold as clay.

The chain and lock clinked again.

"Now, you, boy . . ." began the woman.

"My name's Jake."

"All right, Jake. Come and stand here. Dave wants to show you something."

Jake let her lead him to the center of the caravan, and stood waiting while she stumped out and down the steps.

"Same as before?" she muttered. "Just let me get this bloody mask off."

"Doesn't weigh what I do," said the man. "You may have to help it along. Put your foot on the step. OK?"

"Right."

They pitched their voices below normal hearing, but Jake caught almost every word. The man came up the steps, sat on the bench and shuffled along until he was directly next to where Jake was standing.

"Ready," he called.

There was the same clank as before, followed by the same groaning rumble, only lasting for a shorter time.

"Hear that?" said the man.

"Yes."

"That's the support legs being wound up, that end of the caravan. She's only raised them a couple of inches, but it means that end of the caravan is resting on nothing now. Get it?"

He had a husky, deep voice like an actor's. He sounded as though he was enjoying himself, frightening Jake.

"Yes," said Jake.

"Right. Now what'll happen if you walk down that way?"

❖ 68

"The caravan will tip over, supposing I'm heavy enough."

"Very good. Want to try it?"

"No."

"Go on. Be a dare."

"I might bump into something."

"I'll tell you. Forward — march!"

Timidly Jake shuffled forward, but seething with rage inside. Talking to him like that! Deliberately he shuffled off course. "Right a bit," purred the man. Jake could feel and hear the open door and the woman standing there. Not far now to the end.

Metal creaked slightly from the doorway. The floor angle changed. The jar of the support legs hitting the ground ran up through his bones. He took his cue and staggered slightly.

"Feel that?" said the man.

"Yes."

"Right. Come back here and it'll happen again, won't it?"

"Yes," whispered Jake.

Though he knew more than they thought he did he was still mystified, and though he was aware they were trying to frighten him he couldn't help being frightened. He shuffled back and felt the floor tilt to its proper angle.

"Right," said the man. "When we leave here we're going to wind those legs right up. Then I'm going to throw a switch outside which connects to a couple of butane cylinders which are stored in a rack under the floor, straight below your granddad's bed. There's another switch, a rocker switch, in the circuit. If that switch is rocked far enough, like it might be by some stupid boy wandering round inside here and tipping the van over, then whoomp! Up goes the butane, just like a bomb, and what we have is a nasty little caravan accident to show to anybody who comes asking. Course, by the time they got here your granddad wouldn't have that chain on his leg, and the struts'd be wound down, and there wouldn't be any burned up bits of rocker switch for anybody to find . . . got it?"

"Yes," whispered Jake. It was a scene in a play. Both of them were acting — the man to scare, Jake to be scared. But he was scared too, for real.

"Clever boy," said the man. "Someone'll bring you tea in about an hour. Be good."

The caravan tilted as he strode to the door and settled again as he climbed out. The padlock rattled. The struts rumbled up. Silence, apart from the flap of the wind and the grind of the sea.

"Oh, Granpa!" whispered Jake.

"Sorry about this, Jake. Come down this way. There's a bench just across from my bunk."

Jake found it and settled, automatically reaching out a hand as he did so to take Granpa's. Granpa's grip was firm enough, but his flesh was like clay.

"You're cold!" said Jake.

"Can't seem to get warm. Trouble is I don't get any exercise, and that makes me horrid constipated beside. Have they gone?"

Granpa spoke all but the last three words in a louder voice than usual, but they were a whisper. Jake cocked his head and listened. The wind nudged at the thin walls of the caravan, producing a series of slow, faint booms almost too deep to hear. The sea muttered at its rocks. Jake tuned these noises out and caught the light whimper of cloth on cloth — a sleeve brushing the body of an anorak, perhaps. He shook his head and cupped his hand to his ear. Granpa's grip tightened to show he had understood.

"I don't think we need worry too much, Jake," he said. "All we've got to do is sit quiet and not annoy them. I've no idea what they're up to, but the whole setup makes me think they don't want to hurt us and they'll let us go when it's over. Wearing masks when they come in here is a good sign, for instance. So I'm lying quiet, and so are you."

"Not much I could do," said Jake, finding it a strange relief to continue to turn his fear and shock into acted feebleness. That way he could push them outside his real self and use them as a mask. He wasn't helpless. He'd never been helpless. If these people thought he was, that was their bad luck.

"How did you find me?" said Granpa.

"We went to the newspaper office, and they told us about the old man in the warehouse, and he said he'd told you about this place. We went to Sloughby and Penbottle first. Martin wanted to try his new bike on some real hills."

"New bike? Ah, that explains how you got here. I'd been wondering. Tell me now, what did you make of Penbottle? I wasn't going to bother with Sloughby for the moment. Story's a bit too literary for my taste."

He was still speaking in an artificially loud voice. Jake copied him as he explained about the pele, and the way the old cottager's story differed from Mr. Smith's. Granpa helped him spin things out by asking questions like a cross-examining lawyer, but under the sharpness Jake could sense strain and exhaustion. They finished Penbottle and were moving on to Sloughby when Jake caught another movement from outside. It seemed to dwindle. Low voices spoke, some distance away, and faded down the hill.

"They've gone," said Jake, relaxing.

"Thought they would," said Granpa in his normal voice. "Couldn't afford to hang around long — everything they do goes to show they've got no spare hands, and they're in a hurry. I'd never have stumbled on them the way I did if there were enough of them to keep a proper watch."

"What happened?"

"I got off the bus at the main road. Came down the lane a bit — you can see there used to be a village there, but all the houses have gone. But there's the hummocks of the old mine-workings in some scrubland over to the right so I pottered across to have a look at them. Nothing there, but I took it into my head to climb the tip and have a look out to sea, and once I was there it didn't seem worth going all the way back to the lane. There's a steep sort of sheep path running down that side of the tip and coming out behind some derelict buildings, so I came down that way. It was a bit of a scramble, but I made it. Heard a hacksaw going in the big shed, so I poked my nose in. Coming from that side their sentry didn't spot me."

"Sentry? We were crossing a bridge when a man who sounded like a schoolmaster came and stopped us. He said something about insurance and the buildings being dangerous."

"They tried that one on me. They also said they were doing industrial archaeology, but I was fool enough to let on that I knew a bit about mining and I could see that whatever they were up to, it wasn't that. Next thing the man they call Jack was pointing a gun at me. Brought me up here, and I've been here ever since. Didn't tell them about sending you cards, because I hoped you'd get onto the police and get them to look for me. Never dreamed you'd come yourself."

"Martin bought this bike."

"That explains everything."

"What *were* they doing in the shed, Granpa?"

"Don't know. They'd rigged a screen across it halfway down. Most of them were in behind there. There was one man using a workbench over on the left, and Jack and one of the girls were unpacking something from a crate. Long, thin bit of metal. Can't think what, unless it was a helicopter rotor arm."

"A helicopter!"

"Maybe. Maybe not. Anyway, that's as far as I got."

"I don't understand."

"No more do I."

"We did go to the police, Granpa. I mean, they came to us, but then — anyway, they're helping us look for you, and we promised Sergeant Abraham we'd keep in touch with her. So when we go missing — we didn't tell her exactly what we were doing today, but she knew we'd gone to the newspaper office, so she'll find Mr. Smith, and he'll tell her about how excited we got about his ghost stories, and we talked to several people near Sloughby and at Penbottle, so she'll know we must have come here too."

"That's not bad," said Granpa. "They should be able to trace me on the bus, too. I chatted to one or two people."

He sounded strangely low and dispirited about it, though. No wonder, after all he'd been through, and was still going through.

"Is there really a bomb under your bed, Granpa?"

"I don't think so, Jake. Too much of a risk for them. We had a bit of a gale a couple of nights ago, and twice I thought the caravan was going over, but they didn't come to check."

"I don't think so either. That man was putting it on, like a horror movie."

"Yes. On the other hand they must have done something. They went to a lot of trouble, setting this up. Two of them spent most of one evening on it. They started off by screwing up the windows but when they got to the big one that end they found they'd nothing to screw to. So they had a palaver and fitted me with this leg-iron. Then they went out and had another palaver and spent a good hour mucking around outside. They certainly fixed up something. In the end they came in and told me this story about the butane cylinders and gave me a demonstration of the seesaw effect like the one they gave you. My guess is that they've wired up a rocker switch all right, but they've connected it to some sort of alarm down at the hotel."

"Yes, I see. He was sort of telling the truth, I thought, but not all of it. That might fit . . . is there a window that still opens, Granpa?"

"Only the big one at the front. That was the one they had trouble with."

"I could reach that, I think."

"I doubt it, Jake. You were a good three feet short of it when the van tilted."

"The woman put her foot on the step. He told her to. I heard him, and I heard the step creak."

"Umm. Not good enough. You don't know how hard she pressed. A few inches can make a lot of difference in these leverage problems."

"But —"

"That's enough for the moment, Jake. I'm a bit tired, I'm afraid. This whole business has got me down, and the shock of seeing you walk in — yes, I'm a bit tired."

He sounded it. Jake sat for a while, gently rubbing the loose-skinned icy hand between his palms, but no warmth seemed to come. When Granpa withdrew it and slid it under his bedclothes Jake stood up and began to explore the caravan, working systematically from roof to floor, so that he knew precisely where every obstacle and projection was. On the upper bunk he found another couple of blankets, which he tucked over Granpa, who mumbled his thanks sleepily. Apart from that there was nothing encouraging. The windows this end were completely firm. The storage spaces were all empty. There was a small table and a couple of stools, and beyond them — about as far as he dared explore — the tiny sink and cooker. He went back to the bench and sat down.

He was still there, chilly and worried, when he heard voices outside again. The support legs grumbled and the padlock clicked.

"Teatime," said a new voice, a woman's, sharp and mocking through the slight muffle of her stocking mask. "Wakey wakey, Mr. Uttery. It'll be too dark to eat any minute now."

Granpa groaned and sat up. The wickerwork of a basket creaked as it was put on the table. Paper rustled. She came further along.

"There's your ration, Mr. Uttery. You come and eat at the table, Jake. Can you manage without help?"

"I expect so," whispered Jake, and he allowed himself to be led to a chair and settled in it.

"Right?" she asked. "Then I'll get your bed ready. Hey! Where've those blankets gone? There was a couple —"

"I put them on Granpa," said Jake. "He's icy cold. You feel."

"I'm all right," said Granpa irritably, in exactly the tone he used when Mum fussed about his health. The thought of Mum reminded Jake of something else.

"What about that time on Exmoor?" he said.

"What's Exmoor got to do with it?" said the woman.

"There's a standing stone up there," said Jake. "Some people say they've seen a huge shape walking round and round it under the moon, croaking as it goes. Granpa went to look for it and got pneumonia. He nearly died. You mustn't let him get cold."

"I'm all right, I tell you," said Granpa. "Your mother took it into her head to make a fuss, that's all. And it was probably only a pony."

"Ponies don't croak," said Jake.

"Let me feel your hand," said the woman.

She stood for a moment, sucking her breath meditatively between her lips, then went to the door.

"Tim," she said. "Remember those old stone bed-heaters Terry wanted for his junk shop — in that cupboard on the back landing?"

"Uh-huh."

"Fetch a couple of them up, will you. Better make it four."

"What's the fuss?"

"The old boy's chilled off. I don't like it. I had a neighbor, once, died of hypothermia. I'll get some water hot. Oh, and a sleeping bag for the boy, right?"

"Right."

Jake sat munching at a sausage roll which had been frozen and not quite fully thawed, but he found he was hungry enough not to mind the little crunching crystals in its middle. There's only one of them now, he thought, and it's almost dark. He listened to the woman's movements. She sounded strong and brisk. She was working a little hand pump to fill the kettle and a saucepan. A match grated and the gas began to wuffle. Nobody said anything till the man came back and dumped four solid objects on the floor by the sink.

"Weigh a ton," he said. "Think of servants having to cart those up six flights."

"Dead practical," said the woman. "You kept them in the bedrooms and took boiling water round to fill them. The heat goes into the stone, so you don't lose any, but you don't scorch yourself. Water'll be hot in a couple of minutes."

He must have made some kind of signal to her, because she left the stove and followed him out of doors. Again they thought they'd pitched their voices below Jake's hearing, but hadn't.

"You serious about hypothermia?" he said.

"I don't know. I'm not a doctor. It's a possibility, and you heard what the kid said about pneumonia."

"But that means he might die on us!"

"Yes. That's his lookout. We'll do what we can for him, short of mucking up the project. They've cost us all our slack time already, him and the kids."

"You told me no one was going to get hurt. I only came in because of that."

"This is different," she said, speaking in a much gentler voice as though she were coaxing a child to take nasty medicine. "We'll do what we can for him, keep him warm, all that. It's only three days. He should be all right. But it was him coming poking around — it's his lookout, like I said. He might just as easy have fallen down a mine shaft or something. There's my kettle. You get that sleeping bag ready for the kid and take them to the toilet. We've got to get on, unless you want to be working till three again tonight. I'll need your torch to fill the bottles."

They did the rest of their work in silence, apart from brief instructions to their prisoners. The man was much gentler than the woman. Ten minutes later Jake was lying in the sleeping bag, listening to a new argument fading down the hill. Granpa gave a long sigh.

"Are you all right?" said Jake.

"Much better, thanks. I hadn't reckoned on how cold I was getting. You stop noticing after a bit. Aah."

Jake listened to the wind and the sea. Slowly he nibbled his way through a very nice wheat-meal chicken sandwich.

"I don't think there's a bomb," he said suddenly.

"How d'you make that out? Hear something?"

"Yes. The man told the woman she'd promised him no one would get hurt in what they're doing."

"Glad to hear it. I was fretting about you, Jake. And I daresay you'll sleep easier, too."

"How much do those bottles weigh, Granpa?"

"Lord, I don't know. Haven't seen one since I was your age. Five pounds? Six?"

"That means they've put twenty-four pounds more weight down this end of the caravan."

"Ah, I see what you're getting at."

"Look, suppose I got out — not now, much later — she said something about not working till three in the morning — when does it get light?"

"About six. But it won't do, Jake. The one golden rule for people in our position is that you sit tight."

"No, listen. I'm different. They won't hurt *me*, you see. If it goes wrong I'll just say I was worried because you were much worse and I wanted to get them to come and look at you. I've only got to get past the hotel. Then I can walk up to the main road and hitch a lift somewhere. A call box would do. You don't need money to call the police from one."

Granpa said nothing.

"I can do it," said Jake. "That's the whole point — they don't know I can."

This time Granpa sighed, but still said nothing. When Jake had begun talking his plan had only been a suggestion, but now he realized how strongly he wanted to hit back at these people. For a time, after the scuffle in the hotel, they had made him feel really frightened and helpless, and even now they continued to treat him like that. As he'd talked he'd persuaded himself. He could do it. He'd show them he could. The question whether it was worth doing could wait.

"Where's the water tank?" said Granpa suddenly.

"I don't know. Why?"

"I thought you might have heard a pipe gurgling, or something."

"I'll try, shall I?"

"Wait a moment. There's a kettle and two saucepans, I wonder whether there's a bucket."

"Yes. Under the sink. You mean fill them up too and bring them down this end? They would each weigh about ten pounds."

"Say you can get two of them down here. Twenty pounds. Say the water tank's level with the sink — that's halfway between the axle and the far end, roughly, so taking twenty pounds from there is the same as taking ten from the far end. That makes thirty. Add my water bottles — say fifty in all. If there's anything left in the tank you can pump it out . . . That ought to do it, unless we get a gust of wind at the wrong moment."

"We could say the wind blew it over."

"We'd have a lot of spilled water to explain. Besides, we aren't really dead certain . . ."

"Dead certain what?"

"Nothing. You really want to try this, Jake?"

"Yes."

"All right. If it was anyone else, I'd say no. But I don't think you'll come to any harm."

"Shall I try that tank now?"

"No. There'll be someone round to check, I shouldn't wonder. You see if you can go to sleep. I'll wake you."

"How will you know what the time is?"

"When you've lived my kind of life, you do know. See if you can sleep."

"OK."

It was surprisingly easy, at first. He was deep asleep until a groan woke him — no, not a groan, but the rumble of the support legs being lowered. The second woman came in and refilled the water bottles from a can she'd brought. She said very little. Granpa mumbled his thanks in a slurred voice.

"What's the time?" said Jake.

"Time you were asleep," she said like a nurse in a ward, then added, "Time I was, too."

Jake could hear the exhaustion in her voice, and the tension below the exhaustion. They must be under a strain, too, he thought. Worse than us. Except they chose it.

When she'd gone he dozed, woke, and dozed again. The wind nagged at his half-conscious mind. He thought of it bustling round the broken top of Penbottle Pele and hurling across the bare slopes of Sloughby, and then he was dreaming and it became the rush of air past the pillion of the BMW as Martin drove on a frenzied errand which had to be finished in three days . . .

"Jake?"

"Uh?"

"If you're going, now's the time."

"Are you all right, Granpa? I thought you were just acting when that woman came."

"I'm having a bit of a down, but I'll do. Expect it's only worry about you."

"I'll be all right."

"Yes. It's a good chance. We've got to take it. Not just

for us, Jake. We've got a duty to society. If it were just for us I wouldn't let you go."

Jake grunted as he swung from his bunk. He hadn't thought of it like that. Two minutes later he was working the little pump at the sink, and trying to listen to the suck and gurgle which might tell him where the main tank was.

6

JAKE WAS USED to seesaws. When he'd been much smaller he'd taught himself to walk along the one in the school playground and enjoyed the kick of that strange moment when his own weight tilted the plank the other way, so that he was suddenly walking not up but down. Sighted children keep their balance while they do this by watching the unmoving flats and uprights of the solid world around them, but for Jake it had been a matter of learning to sense through the soles of his feet the first tremble of change and adjusting to it as it came.

It was like that now. He was holding his stick in his right hand and his shoes in his left and inching forward across the last stretch of the caravan floor. He'd gone quite confidently at first, but now, in the part beyond where he'd reached during Dave's demonstration, he was suddenly conscious that every fresh inch was taken on the basis of pure guesswork. It was only a guess that Dave had been kidding about the bomb. His sums were mostly guesses too — the water tank might run right back across the axle, and the axle mightn't be dead in the middle of the caravan, and the wind . . .

Each gust made the caravan quiver. Each quiver was like the tremble that would come when the whole thing began to tilt. He slid his foot forward and slowly swung his weight onto it, paused, and slid the other foot. He tried to drain all his senses into his soles, but they were half numb with the chill of the floor. The wind buffeted against the glass in front of him, very near. He let his cane reach a little further and it tapped on metal. He tucked it under his left arm, stretched out his hand, and felt the chill of glass.

This gust was fiercer than most, and as it lulled Jake felt the whole metal box he was in settle slightly. He didn't even dare step back, but stood tense until the next gust seemed to lift the caravan again. The movement hadn't been the first stirring of weight round the axle then, but the wind actually helped him, holding the caravan at its proper angle. He took a quick, short step, slid his hand down to the window rim and along it and found the catch. He twisted it and pushed. The glass, hinged at the top, swung open.

It was like loosing a kenneled dog. The wind rushed hooting through the gap and rampaged round the caravan. The whole box bucked at that first impact and, as he pushed the window further, felt as though it were trying to take off like a kite. Hurriedly he dropped his shoes through the gap, swung a leg to the sill, and twisted himself over, letting go with his hands the moment his feet were swinging down. His ankle banged on the tow bar, tilting him face first onto trampled grass. Shuddering with the release of tension he reached for the window and pushed it to. There was no way of latching it.

His stick was still in his hand, clutched tight by instinct. He used it to find his shoes, then put them on and stood shivering in the hissing salt wind. The outer layers of his body protested at the onslaught of cold, but before the fit was over he started to move, zigzagging down the slope, guided by the thin, continuous booming where the wind pressed and released the flanks of the other caravans. The loom and boom of them guided him between the gaps, while to his left, giving him his general direction, the North Sea growled and grunted on the shore and every now and then, where a wave slashed into some cleft of rocks, yelped like a huge ghost hound.

Beyond the last line of caravans the wind came unhindered. In its first impact it felt as though it were trying to bundle Jake off his path, but he leaned into it and walked steadily down, though his ankle still hurt where it had banged the tow bar. The wind, so apparently unfriendly, was a real help, picking out details round him in a series of hisses and booms and whistles. When he reached the bottom of the slope he could hear it nagging at the bridge, a few yards to his right, and once there he was able to put out a hand and grasp the guardrail without groping. Below him a middle-sized stream — it must be Annerton Dike — muttered its last few yards towards the sea. On its far bank the path, deep rutted with car tracks, climbed steeply. Jake went carefully up and halted at the edge of the cobbles.

Would there be any light coming from the hotel? Granpa had said that the night was pitch dark, but he hadn't actually been able to reach a window which looked out in this direction. Would it be best to cross the seawall and scramble along the rocks out of sight from the hotel windows? No. The tide was up, and the smaller harbor waves were sloshing with a regular sound along a straight unbroken line, which must be the wall itself. There was no way through there. Someone at last must have become maddened by the tap of the halyard on the yacht's mast and had tightened it so that now it whined shrilly, a gap in the teeth of the wind. That meant that the boat was something to do with the enemy.

What about a dog? Nothing had barked when the BMW drove up that afternoon. That didn't prove anything. They might have a guard dog which they let roam around at night. Hell, Jake thought, I've got to go on. I'd better act feeble for a bit, so that if they do see me I can say I came to look for Martin.

He stepped forward at an old man's shuffle, wavering his stick in wide arcs above the cobbles and from time to time groping in front of his face. Deliberately he chose a crooked and uncertain-seeming path, but let it take him towards the front wall of the hotel, where he thought there might be shadow even if a light was on. The thud of the wind on the building came clearly through the sea roar. The window where the curtain had flapped that afternoon was now closed, but the wind had risen enough to set up a new vibration in a length of guttering so that it complained with a shallow, throbbing note. Jake's cane met the stonework of the hotel's corner within six inches of where he expected it.

He paused. The temptation was to make a dash for it. The longer he doddered about in front of the building the more chance there was of being spotted. But if he was seen moving quickly and confidently, then the rest of his story, about coming to get help for Granpa, wouldn't work. He forced himself to shuffle hesitantly along, keeping close to the hotel wall, where at least he might be missed by anyone glancing out of an upstairs window. He hesitated again at the front door, trying to look as though he was making up his mind whether to try here or to go on round to the side door which Mr. Andrews had used. Nothing moved. The space in front of the hotel had nothing in it to muddle the rush of the wind.

Martin's bike — the BMW. That should have been standing here. They'd hidden it, of course, in case anyone came and asked whose it was. They hadn't any right! It was strange how angry this made him. The other things they'd done were much worse — taking people prisoner, chaining Granpa to his bed and letting him get ill and not fetching a doctor — but those had only made Jake afraid. Mucking around with Martin's bike was different. Martin loved it so much. They hadn't any right! When I get to Newcastle, he thought . . . he clenched his hand round his stick as if it were a weapon. Then he thought, come on, you've got to get to Newcastle first.

He dropped the invalid shuffle as soon as he was round the corner and strode firmly half-left towards the cliff, misjudging the angle slightly so that he reached it where the cobbles swung off round the back of the hotel and were separated from the cliff road by a brick outbuilding. He tapped his way back along the front of this and started to climb.

The road surface was very rough, churned down the middle with the passage of caravans and holidaymakers' cars and lorries. Jake had to choose between the outer edge, above the steadily increasing drop, or the edge by the cliff to his right where the path was loose with fallen rubble and where the occasional jagged boulder stuck out to bar his way. Even so it was obviously safer than the outside edge, so he probed his way carefully up with his stick, still moving as quietly as possible, though he thought that by now he must be well out of earshot of the sleepers in the hotel. The wind swirled and eddied against the cliff above him, breaking into sudden downdrafts and strange little pockets of calm. The surf roar changed its note as he climbed; now, through its thunder against the rocks, Jake could hear the movement of the whole reach of sea beyond, with the ceaseless hiss of the wind along the wave ridges and the long mutter of marching waters below. And now he could feel the altered run of the wind where, only a few feet above him, it ceased to drive against the barrier of the cliff but bucketed across the jagged edge and roared inland. Nearly there.

Jake stopped. It was the natural thing to do, at the point between one stage of his journey and the next. Perhaps it was natural in another way too — an instinct of care inherited from far-back ancestors, hunters and sometimes hunted. He didn't notice that his head had tilted slightly and his ears were wary for slighter sounds than the uproar of the gale. They heard nothing, though he was standing in one of the sudden pockets of calm. He shrugged again and was about to move on when the wind whipped brusquely sidelong down the cliff face. Briefly but unmistakably it brought him the smell of a cigarette.

It was only the faintest tang, almost smothered by the salt and seaweed, but it was there. It was smoke, too, and not the stale remains of a damp fag-end. Jake stayed where he was, waiting and listening, while the wind blew violently the other way, stilled, and slammed in again from the sea. At last it chose to gust along the cliff and the smoke was still there. The night was colder than ever, and the surface of Jake's flesh was ready to break into shivers, but fear kept him still.

The man coughed. Jake's ears had been straining after minute fragments of sound; the noise, so near and violent, almost made him drop his stick. The man swore at himself, stamped his feet and slapped his arms against his sides. For a moment Jake thought he was going to come down the road, and of course he'd have a torch in order to pick his way, but he fell back into silence. Jake realized that the enemy were short of men and could only afford one sentry, so naturally they'd put him up here, at the only entrance to the bay.

It was tempting to stay, to look for a boulder by the road and crouch behind it, in the hope that the man would have to go down to wake the next sentry and so pass safely by, but Jake knew this wouldn't do. He'd long ago learned that blind children are no good at hide-and-seek — no good at either half of the game. In fact they are better at seeking than hiding, because touch and smell and hearing have a chance there. But to hide you need to see, because that's the only way of knowing whether you can be seen. Very carefully he started to pick his way back down the cliff road, towards the hotel. Now that he knew there was a listener so close it seemed harder to move in silence than it had been when he'd climbed the road thinking that all the enemy were behind him, asleep in their beds.

Surely there must be a way round the sentry! As soon as he thought he was out of the man's earshot Jake stopped to explore the rock face on his left. He could hear the wind's hiss among the grass stems at the top, a good twenty feet above him. The rock itself seemed smooth and sheer. Jake shook his head and stole on down. The best bet would be to wait by the brick shed he'd found at the bottom and hope that when the sentry went for his relief there'd be time to get up the road while it was unguarded. He hadn't reached the bottom when he heard the hotel door slam.

He crouched so that a fall wouldn't jar him too much and scuttered down onto the cobbles. As he raced along the front of the shed he could hear the footsteps coming towards the corner of the hotel, and reaching the end just as he ducked round into the backyard and flattened himself against the inner wall. The stride of the newcomer didn't falter. He wore nailed shoes which struck grittily on the cobbles. He yawned as he passed the courtyard entrance. A couple of minutes later the other man, wearing gumboots, came back down the road. He was muttering about something as he passed. The hotel door opened and shut. Jake gave a long, tired sigh.

What now?

All of a sudden he'd had enough of action. He'd proved to himself that he could do as much as any sighted boy could have done — more, because a sighted boy would have stumbled into the arms of the sentry. Wasn't that enough? Couldn't he go back now to the warmth of his bunk and the comfort of Granpa's presence and say that he tried, and it wasn't any good?

He started to sigh again, but on the indrawn breath he was suddenly aware of the faint tang of petrol. It wasn't surprising. This shed was probably a garage — in fact very likely Martin's bike had been wheeled away inside there. The thought of it made his anger flare inside him again, not warming his shuddering flesh at all but somehow warming his mind. There must be another way past the sentry. What had Granpa said? ". . . didn't seem worth going all the way back to the lane . . . sheep path running down that side of the tip . . . coming out behind some derelict buildings . . . bit of a scramble . . ."

I'll try that, thought Jake. I expect they've locked the shed for the night.

He allowed himself one more good shiver, then made his way across the cobbles to the corner of the hotel, turned sharply away, and walked with the sea roar on his left until his stick touched a scraping barrier, a low cement wall by the feel of it. Yes, coming with Martin he'd have started a little further out from the hotel front. He moved crabwise a couple of yards into the buffeting wind until his stick found the gap in the wall where the path began. It felt like the one he remembered, slimy and rutted, with patches of loose shingle in the worst hollows. It dipped almost to the level of the muttering harbor surf, then rose to the point where the schoolmaster had stopped them. There ought to be a bridge soon.

There was. The wind caught a handrail on either side. Water tinkled below. It was almost a replica of the bridge into the caravan field, but something was different, an inexplicable tiny whine in the wind, low down, too regular to be anything like a grass-blade. Jake moved forward very slowly with his stick held lightly between his fingertips, probing almost at ground level. Halfway across he felt a slight resistance, a hard line running from side to side of the bridge only a few inches above the timbers. He stopped and explored it delicately from end to end. A trip wire, he thought — connected to an alarm bell or something.

Low though it was it seemed an extraordinary barrier. Once more Jake hesitated, listening and smelling the wind, and once more his nostrils brought him a sense of danger. This new smell came in a lull of the storm, a deep, chill, dank odor — not the dankness of decaying vegetation, but the dankness of caves, lifeless and still. After a while Jake decided that it was only the smell of the stream that slid beneath the bridge, and only alarming because all his senses were stretched to respond to anything strange in the night. Come on, he whispered to himself. You're wasting time.

He forced himself to step carefully across the trip wire and off the bridge, but the dank smell lingered in his mind like the shreds of a different nightmare. Or perhaps it was the wire that had frightened him more than he realized, by showing him that the enemy were as careful as they were dangerous.

Beyond the bridge the path rose steeply towards a big, low building. The wind burrowed at gaps in its roof and flapped a piece of corrugated iron to and fro along a rusty nail, making it screech with metal pain. Something tall and thin rose nearby — probably a chimney stack — and there seemed to be other, smaller buildings or remains of buildings over to the right, close under the incurving cliff. But beyond the big shed, and higher than the cliffs themselves, rose a large shapeless mass; the wind tore at a steep-sided pile, giving out a long-drawn hiss as each gust scrabbled at bushes and brambles along its lower flanks. Annerton tip, of course, whose weight had caused the disaster. Good place for a picnic, Martin had said. Looked like an enormous burial mound.

There was something else about the tip, not just its bigness, its unmoved mass in the swirl and tumult of the night. Jake felt that even on the stillest of days he would have known it was there, would have been aware of its sheer mass piled on the groaning rocks, almost as though it were something more than a heap of unwanted rubble, something that had been deliberately built so that its weight could hold down, imprison, trap forever . . . trap what?

Jake shook his head, remembering his stupid fear of the smell of the stream. It's because I'm so tired, he thought. I think things which aren't there. I must get on. At least the tip was a good sound-beacon, full of rustles and hisses to guide him on the next stage of his journey.

He never made that journey.

The last stretch of track leveled out onto a little plateau below the tip and the cliffs, where the buildings stood.

Jake moved carefully towards the front of the shed, probing all the time for trip wires, and to his surprise found that the big doors were open. This isn't so good, he thought. There may be another sentry here, if this is where the work's being done. He knew the doors were open by the sound of the wind swooshing into the hollow cave of the shed instead of beating against a blank surface. When he reached the near leaf he was relieved to find that there was a reason for it's not being shut — it was leaning all askew, half off its hinges, and was far too large and heavy for even a team of men to shift, and probably would have fallen to bits if they'd tried.

Jake felt his way to the outer edge of the door and stood listening, and breathing in slow, considering lungfuls, so as not to miss the faintest wisp of scent. He smelled nothing besides the wild sea smell and a little oily metal such as might belong to any workshop; he heard nothing except the waves and the racketing wind; all the same he was afraid. There was something evil about this place. Ever since he'd crossed the last stream the nature of his fear had changed; before that the bay and the cliffs and the sea had been neutral, and the storm had even been an ally; danger had only come from Jack Andrews and Jeannie and their friends. Now everything was dangerous, the wind, the shed, the looming tip, the ground under his feet. Jake shook his head, clicked his tongue softly on his palate to protest against his own stupidity, and walked quickly across the front of the shed. As he did so he became aware that the wind wasn't booming unhindered into the cave of it, but was having to swirl round a large thing that blocked half the entrance — a truck, he thought; the moment he'd decided that, its shape became obvious. Yes, a fair-sized truck.

The far leaf of the doors was completely off its hinges

and only stood at all because it was propped against a pile of loose rubble. Jake went up to this on hands and knees and found that it leveled off about four feet from the ground. He stood on this little platform and listened to the wind picking out the details of the slope above him. He prodded with his stick for the edge of the bushes he could hear a little to his left, checked that the space in front of him was clear of any arching spray of bramble, and stepped onto the tip itself. As he did so the world changed.

It was as though a bell jar had been lowered over him to cut him off from the roaring wind and the roaring sea; beyond the imaginary glass they threshed away, but inside it there was only this pocket of terror, the gas he breathed, the stillness in his ears, the chill along his skin — all terror. He stepped so sharply back onto the pile of rubble that he almost fell down the slope of it. The noise of wind and sea came back into his ears and the sea smell into his nostrils, but his shudders were not caused by the cold. He slashed stupidly at the space where he'd stood as if a solid shape might be crouched there, but the thin stick whistled through air. He shook his head and clicked his tongue again, but now crossness at his own stupidity wasn't enough to force him on. Sharp in his mind came the tangling clutch of briars, his own body trapped and helpless on the flank of the tip, starving there, or being found by the vengeful enemy. He almost whimpered at the idea of it. And what would they do to Granpa? He remembered hearing on the radio about some Irish kidnappers who had started to knock out their hostage's teeth to make him do what they wanted. Granpa was proud of his good teeth. The important thing was to get Granpa away . . . If only it weren't for that chain. If only . . .

Just as though somebody had whispered in his ear Jake remembered other things Granpa had said. ". . . heard a hacksaw going . . . man using a workbench over on the left . . ." A hacksaw! If Jake could find that! Say ten minutes back to the caravan, ten minutes to saw through the chain, ten minutes back here. They could climb the tip together.

With another part of his mind he knew perfectly well that Granpa might be too weak to do any such thing. He mightn't even be able to climb out through the caravan window. And if the tip had been a scramble to come down . . .

But Jake knew too that he was, at the moment, quite incapable of climbing the tip alone. Not allowing himself another moment to think more reasonably about the plan he turned and felt his way down the tumbled stones. As he rounded the door the wind seemed to be trying to blast him into the shed, but he remembered about trip wires and tested his way through the gap between the truck and the doorpost. The shed was quite a bit wider than its doors, so he had to feel his way round by the front wall. Some loose sheet metal, quite new and rust-free by the feel of it, was stacked in the corner. If he unsettled that the clang of its fall might be enough to alert the sentry on the cliff top — the wind was that way. Gingerly Jake inched past it and along the side wall until his stick, wavering in front of him, tapped lightly on a vertical strut. Following it up he found it supported a wooden surface, greasy with oil and rough with metal filings. This was the workbench. Jake moved along it, systematically exploring its surface with his fingertips, but found only a few odd bits of metal, a heavy hammer, a vice and a single large chunk of machined steel that felt like part of an engine. What do workmen do with their tools at the end of the day, he thought. Put them in a toolcase, or hang them on the wall. He worked back leaning across the bench and running his fingers up and down the brickwork beyond. Yes, they'd nailed a batten up and fastened clips to it to hold things — a matched set of spanners — three screwdrivers — something complicated he didn't recognize — ah! . . .

Four or five feet away, behind Jake and to his left, a voice muttered "Run! Oh, get on! It's coming! It's coming out of that crack! Run, damn you!"

Nothing moved. With his hand round the frame of the hacksaw Jake froze, suddenly once more in the bell jar of terror. Most of his mind shrieked to run, but his legs wouldn't move, and then another part of his mind told him that he knew that sort of mutter. The man was talking in his sleep, the way Martin often did. There was a man asleep in the cab of the lorry. They couldn't afford a waking sentry, so they let him sleep up here. Perhaps the trip wire sounded in his cab . . .

Slowly the bell jar lifted again and Jake began to unfreeze, but didn't dare pull the hacksaw from the wall in case the clip clicked. He decided to count to a hundred to let the man get back out of the shallows of his nightmare and into deep sleep, but he was still in the twenties when the man gave a violent snort and then swore in a waking voice. Jake froze again. There was the sharp little click of a torch switch, another short pause, and then the man said "Hey! Who the hell . . ."

As the door handle of the lorry snapped down Jake ran for the open. The door itself touched his shoulder as he passed it. He scuttled with his stick probing at knee level round the leaf of the door, up the pile of rubble, and straight onto the slope of the tip. The man was in the open now too, shouting at the top of his voice. He must have missed Jake's turn round the door for his footsteps thudded a few paces down towards the bridge, but then he stopped, paused, and yelled "Hey! You! Come back!" in a voice which told Jake that the torch beam had caught him.

Jake was only a few feet up the slope when a stone rattled off the rubble pile. A bramble caught at his anorak. He lurched forward to wrench free but his feet slithered under him and he fell. Before he was on his knees a hand closed round his ankle and dragged him bodily back down the slope. Jake was yelling "Let go! Let go!" without noticing. The man was still shouting too. Jake lashed out with his stick at the voice and the shout changed to one of pain as the thin rod slapped into flesh, but the man didn't let go. Instead he jerked violently and for an instant Jake felt himself falling before he thudded into the man's chest and was pinioned by hard arms.

"Let's have a look at you," said the man. "Jesus, it's the blind kid!"

"Let me go!" yelled Jake.

The man laughed.

"Sure," he said. "When you've had a word with Jack."

"I was looking for my brother," said Jake. His pretend sob became real.

"Sure," said the man again. "With a hacksaw, uh?"

Jake hadn't realized he was still gripping the tool. The man spun him round and marched him towards the hotel.

They met Jack Andrews at the point where the path became cobbles.

"What's up, Tony?" he said.

The man who had caught Jake explained. Other footsteps began to arrive across the cobbles.

"What were you doing, Jake?" said Mr. Andrews. On the surface his voice was friendlier than ever, but in its depths Jake could hear the stress building towards an explosion.

"Granpa's worse," said Jake. "I couldn't sleep. I think he's really ill, so I came to look for you, only I got lost . . ."

He sounded as scared as he felt. Nobody ever dreams a blind child might be lying, he thought. But this time . . .

"He'd got the hacksaw off the workbench," said Tony. "When I spotted him he was out of the shed like a rabbit and running up the tip. Like he wasn't blind at all."

"No, Jack, no!" shouted another man.

At the same instant something struck Jake a huge blow on the side of his head. He felt himself beginning to fall and his throat beginning to yell with the shock of pain. Then he felt nothing.

7

T HE ONLY TIMES Jake had ever "seen" anything had come when he had hurt his head — once when he was about five in a playground when a wooden swing had knocked him unconscious and once, a couple of years ago, when an electrician's van had lost its steering and knocked down him and Becky Skipwith while they were walking home from school. Becky had broken both legs, but Jake had been luckier and was only concussed. Both times Jake had been aware, as he came to, that something had happened inside his brain which wasn't seeing, but was like it. There'd been brightnesses, sharp edged but shapeless, with colors in them. They were part of the pain. Fully conscious he found it difficult to make his memory re-create what he had "seen," but they'd been there, unlike the occasional tiresome dream he had in which he could really see — only of course he couldn't, even in the dreams, because his dreaming brain hadn't got any real experience of seeing to work on. The dreams were just his suppressed and unconscious longing to see, coming out in this frustrating way.

Now, though, as he was half aware of angry voices grumbling into agreement, like a dying storm, he "saw" the flashes and the colors. He was dangling head and feet down, over a man's shoulder. The man was walking, and at every step the blood seemed to bounce in the hurt cells of Jake's brain. The wrong side of his head hurt — not the one which had been hit, but the other side. For several paces the colors came and went, and footsteps creaked on pebbles, and the arguing voices dwindled — was one of them Martin's, further, further away, drowning in the sea and the wind? Then there was numbness and silence.

He came to in a quite different place. It began as a dankness and deadness in his nostrils, and the clicks of falling water drops in his ears. He was lying on chilly, slippery earth. His head hurt, still on the wrong side. He realized that he must have fallen badly after the man had hit him and bashed it on something. He felt sick, too. There were a lot of faint echoes. Each time a drip fell it was answered and answered again, so that after lying there a minute or two Jake knew that he was in a widish tunnel, but close to the end of it. The end, in fact, was a nearly flat surface, made of something less echoing than the walls and roof. The other end was out of earshot. Straining, he thought he could hear the mutter of waves, but not the wind. The smell was very peculiar, not strong or unpleasant, but unlike anything else, heavy and wet and lifeless. The air felt as though it hadn't stirred for a hundred years.

There was another noise, even fainter than the sea. Jake couldn't decide whether it was real, or was only an effect of the fall — a low, continuous, throbbing hoot. Sometimes it seemed to be coming from further up the tunnel, sometimes from all round him, and sometimes from inside his head. Once he'd noticed it, it bothered him.

After a while a voice spoke, muffled, as if from the other

side of a wall. Another voice answered. Wood creaked on wood and the sea noise became much louder. Footsteps squelched. A load, light but large, flopped to the floor. The footsteps came nearer.

"How're you feeling?" said a man's voice. "Are you awake?"

It was Dave, the one who'd demonstrated how the caravan tilted. Jake groaned.

"Come off it," said Dave. "You've done us once, playing soft. That won't wash anymore. I've brought you a couple of aspirin. Here. Sit up. I've got a groundsheet for you, too. Every comfort."

Jake allowed himself to be levered into a sitting position. This time his groan was real, stifling all questions. By the time the pain ebbed he was sucking at the dusty sweet pills and listening to more footsteps coming, several people, moving slowly.

"Where's my grandson?" said Granpa's voice. "What have you done with him?"

"He's in here," said one of the women. "There. Shine your torch on him, Terry."

"Jake! Are you all right?"

"My head hurts. They hit me, then I hit it on the ground. It wasn't all their fault."

"Now, listen —"

"Stow it, Mr. Uttery. You brought it on yourselves. Look, Dave's got a rubber mattress for you, and Terry's got your blankets. You lie down now and keep warm, and think yourself bloody lucky that you aren't worse off than you are already."

Granpa drew a breath to argue but let it become a sigh. He seemed to be moving very shakily as they led him to the mattress. While they were covering him with the blankets more voices reached into the tunnel — mainly Mr.

Andrews giving orders in sharp bursts of words. Footsteps again, one set well known.

"Jake!" cried Martin. "Are you all right? I saw him hit you! I saw it!"

"I'm OK," said Jake, automatically making his voice noncommittal in order to balance out Martin's excitement, as if this had been an ordinary family row in the kitchen at home.

"They might have cracked —"

"Shut up," said Mr. Andrews. "Right, Dave. Thanks Helen, thanks Terry. You go back and get a bit of sleep. See the others do, too. Ask Ray to find a sack, fill it with food and drink for three for three days, and then hang about outside, while I lay it on the line to these idiots."

"OK, Jack," said someone.

Their footsteps slopped away over the slimy floor. A door creaked and the sea noise muted.

"Right," said Mr. Andrews. "You go and sit there, Martin, by your grandfather's head, where I can see you both. Put your hands on your knees and don't move them. I'll come over here, by Jake. Now you're all three in the line of my torch. This gun is loaded and its safety catch is off. I promise you that if I have the slightest trouble from any of you I'll shoot Jake's kneecap off."

"But Prop Five —" began Martin.

"Shut up. Can't you see that you've changed all that? I'm not even sorry I hit him. I'm sorry it was him I hit, but it was going to happen to someone. That's the way this sort of stunt goes. You start off telling everybody, including yourself, that nobody's going to get hurt. But if you're honest with yourself you recognize that there's got to be the possibility of people getting hurt — getting killed — innocent people. If you aren't prepared to hurt and kill then you've got no leverage. Of course, you try to set it up so that it doesn't come to that, but the possibility must be there, you get me? Well, now we've reached that point."

He paused for an instant, then spoke more slowly.

"I am prepared to hurt you, if necessary to kill you, and so are most of the others. In a way I'm glad that things have panned out this way, because your fooling around has forced them to recognize that necessity before it comes to the crunch. They've got to face the facts now, instead of in three days' time. That means that if the necessity arises *then*, they won't hesitate."

This was a new Mr. Andrews, neither bluff nor cheerful. He was arguing with himself, proving to himself that what he was doing was right. He was less certain about that than he thought he was.

"Now I'll explain the setup to you," he said. "You're in what I believe is called a drift mine. It's an abandoned tunnel into the cliff. We use it as our explosives store. The explosives are beyond that partition there. Beyond that is another partition, and beyond that is a shed. If you come to it from the outside you think it's a shed built against the cliff. The outer partition looks like all there is, but a panel in it can be moved to let you into the explosives store. Just in the same way another panel in the second partition lets you through into here. We don't use this space, because it's too damp for explosives. Now, listen carefully, because this is the bit you've got to get into your thick heads. The outer partition is wired on an electrical circuit, so that if anybody tries to open the panel or break through without throwing a hidden switch, then the whole explosives store will go up. Four and a half hundredweight of plastic, Mr. Uttery. You know what sort of a bang that'll make. I suppose if you go right up to the end of the tunnel you might live through it, but it'll bring the cliff face down for sure, with you inside. So, then — suppose your friends the police come round — suppose they start nosing about — what do you do? You sit quiet. You don't shout. You don't bang. You just pray they don't notice that outer partition's a dummy. Got it?"

Nobody answered. Instead Granpa said in a low voice, "Why didn't you put me in here in the first place?"

"Because the others weren't ready to recognize the necessity. Instead we had to go through that charade with the caravan. This isn't a charade, I promise you, and they do recognize it now. And I'll tell you why I put you in the caravan instead of down at the hotel — because I didn't want them getting involved with you. I wanted them to have as little to do with you as possible. This is my first go at this kind of stunt. I've been base man, till now, looking after explosives, all that. And we've never messed around with hostages. But I've read the literature, and one thing's for sure from what I've read. If you do find yourself with hostages, you can't afford to build up a relationship with them. That's why, when I go now, I'm not coming back. I'm going to spend the rest of tonight wiring this inner partition into the circuit, so that if you start playing silly bastards with it you'll blow yourselves to bits. Then I'll leave you strictly alone. When we leave, we'll take most of the explosives with us, but we'll leave a couple of pounds still wired up. Then, when we're out there, we'll radio back to shore and tell the cops where to look for you and where to find the safety switch. That'll show we mean business, and it'll also show goodwill, uh? So you get it, you three? You sit tight and you'll come through. You muck about like you've been doing so far and you won't."

"Out there?" said Granpa.

Mr. Andrews had been squatting down to Jake's right, only a few feet away. Now cloth rustled and soles and tendons creaked. His voice rose to standing height.

"Martin'll tell you," he said.

His footsteps squelched towards the partition. Jake hesitated, gulping the damp, tomb-chill air.

"You can't leave Granpa here," he whispered. "Not for three days. He'll get pneumonia, like on Exmoor."

"Yeah," said Martin, caught by the new idea. "That's right. You can't leave him here. He sounds a bit grotty already."

"You haven't got it," said Mr. Andrews in a low, tense voice. "I'm doing the best I can for you. I haven't got any more time. I slept three hours last night, and two hours this, so far. Now I'm going to have to spend an hour wiring up this partition. I've got to keep a clear head, got to keep track of the whole op. I can't afford to go groggy, not getting any sleep. So I'm giving you an hour of that time, when I could have shot the three of you and gone straight back to bed. If your granddad dies, I'm sorry. But it's still if. A bullet is for sure."

"But that's against the propositions!" cried Martin, sounding merely astonished. Jake had no idea what he was talking about.

"Yeah?" said Mr. Andrews. "You know what? I used to think being committed to a cause, really committed, meant that I was ready to die for it. Now I can see I was only halfway there. Being committed means I've got to be ready to kill for it. See you."

His steps moved out towards the sea noise, only to return almost at once. He dumped something heavy and soft close to Jake, said, "That's your rations," and left again. Wood slithered and grated and the sea noise dulled almost below hearing. Once again Jake noticed the curious throbbing hoot that seemed to fill the tunnel; the aspirin had taken the edge off his headache but the sound hadn't changed, so he thought it must be coming from outside his skull. It vanished again when Mr. Andrews started work; it was so faint that even the clink of pliers or the burr of a hand drill was enough to catch the hearing and tune it out.

"What did he mean 'out there'?" said Granpa suddenly.

"I can't tell you. Sorry," said Martin.

"Come off it," said Jake.

"It's against the propositions," said Martin, furious with doubt.

"That means a lot to me," said Jake.

Granpa sighed.

"Out there," he said. "Out in the North Sea somewhere. Are they using a helicopter, Martin?"

"How did you . . ." began Martin, then stopped.

"Listen, Martin, we're all pretty tired and shocked. But in a mess like this we've got to keep our wits about us. It's our only hope. The less we know about what's happening, the more chance there is we'll make a mistake which'll cost us our lives — other people's too, perhaps."

Martin drew his breath to speak and let it out in a gust of frustration.

"Do you believe what he said?" said Granpa. "A cause is something you have to be prepared to kill for?"

"No," snapped Martin.

"I've never killed anybody, that I know of," said Granpa. "I suppose, as an engineer in the war, I helped to kill people, but I've never actually pulled the trigger with my sights on a man. I thought I was going to have to once. There was a tribal uprising against the government and both sides got out of hand, whole villages wiped out, neutral ones as well. Some of us fetched up at a missionary settlement and laid on some ramshackle defenses, and the only bunch of thugs who came our way — they were government ones — decided to leave us alone. I think I would have pulled the trigger then, though there weren't many causes around. Just my own life, and a couple of hundred villagers and a few Baptist missionaries."

"That's different," said Martin.

Mr. Andrews hammered something into the partition. The tunnel boomed like the inside of a drum. Jake thought he heard the echoes answering from its furthest end.

"What's a drift mine, anyway?" said Martin, obviously trying to push the talk away from his own miseries. "Is this part of the pit where the ghost is?"

"Don't you remember?" said Jake. "Mr. Smith told us. It's where the coal seam comes to the surface and you can get at it sidelong."

"That's right," said Granpa. "But there are a lot of faults in the rocks round here, places where there've been slips, so that the seams of coal break off and start at another level. The miners probably stopped digging here when they reached a fault line. The main pit's further inland. They'd have sunk a shaft to get at that part of the seam."

He paused. He sounded very tired, and Jake guessed he was only talking in order to let Martin think his own way through.

"How far does this part go?" asked Jake. "It sounded pretty deep."

"Could be several hundred yards," said Granpa, "but it isn't likely. If it's an early mine, it'll probably branch into two or three main tunnels, with a whole lot of short side passages, like cells. They call it monks' working, not because of the cells, but because most of the mines up here belonged to the monasteries. Very wasteful way of winning coal. To stop the roof coming down they left more between the cells than they took out. Probably left as much as two-thirds of the coal behind."

He paused again. The water drips marked the tunnel more clearly, now that Jake had been told what kind of shape it might have. The main passage curved raggedly to the right. Some of the irregularities were the openings of cells. One, with a couple of syncopated drips in it, opened only a few yards up on the left. Jake wondered whether it wasn't time to put a little more pressure on Martin, not directly but obliquely.

"How's your head?" said Granpa. "If I'd thought that might happen I wouldn't have let you go."

"It's better," said Jake. "One of them gave me some aspirin. It hurt a lot when it happened."

Martin stirred but said nothing.

"I think we'd all better get some sleep," said Granpa. "They've made me quite comfortable. I've got one of those inflatable rubber things. What about you two?"

"Hang on a minute," said Martin in a low voice. "Has he gone, Jake?"

The hammer answered before Jake could, a series of light taps in groups of four or five, with pauses in between.

"He's stapling a bit of cable along the other partition," said Jake, "I bet he couldn't hear anything through that."

"Damn," said Martin. "I've been sitting under a drip."

"Come up here," said Jake. "They brought me a tarpaulin to sit on and nothing's fallen on it yet. There's room for you."

Martin came groping along and settled down. Time measured itself in drips and echoes. The boys shared a sandwich. Granpa's breathing slowed and deepened. At last came the chink of tools being gathered together, movement of wood on wood and the final dulling of the sea surge.

"He's gone," said Jake.

"Shh," whispered Martin. "Are you awake, Granpa?"

No answer.

"Don't wake him up," said Martin. "Let him stay that way. I've got to tell you first, Jake. I've made a mess of things."

"So've I."

"No. You brought them out into the open. I was furious with you when it happened, but when he hit you . . . listen, do you know who these people are?"

"No. They haven't told us anything."

"They're the GR headquarters. Jack Andrews made the bombs which the Epping Five used. Made them himself. Here."

"How do you know?"

"He told me."

"Told you!"

Jake was frightened. If Mr. Andrews was prepared to tell Martin things like that, things that might send him to prison for thirty years, then perhaps he didn't mean to let them go after all.

"They took me off to a room to question me," said Martin. "On the way there I heard one of them use a bit of GR jargon, so as soon as I got the chance I let Jack know that I knew the Propositions."

"Come again."

"The Propositions. They're not exactly oaths you swear when you join. They're . . . well, they're propositions. You have to give them total assent. They're about what the world ought to be like, and how we're going to get it there."

"How do *you* know them?"

"That's what's been screwing me up," said Martin. "You see, you go in steps. You've got to assent to each Proposition before you're told the next one. If you can't assent you're allowed to withdraw. So the first Proposition of all has to be about secrecy. You assent to that, and they don't tell you any more for a couple of months at least. They watch you, test you, and if you come through they tell you Props Two to Five. Prop Five is the no-violence one."

"Bombing motorways is violent."

"It's the building motorways which is violent. Bombing them is only trying to undo that — and GR went to fantastic trouble to see no one got hurt. That's how the Epping Five got themselves caught. But Prop One's what's been bugging me — I just don't talk about GR, even to you. I bet you'd no idea how far I was into it."

"Well, I knew you'd been to demos, and you were collecting for the trial . . ."

"Yeah, but those are outside things . . . Once you're into GR you find it's a darned big organization. There were twenty-seven in our Portsmouth group, for instance, but only two of them were in contact with the next group in, and we didn't know who those two were. When you move inward you're told more Propositions. And so on, further and further in, till you get to Jack and the Epping Five and three or four more bods at the center. It's not such a coincidence our stumbling in like this — I mean, supposing someone about my age had come along here, there'd be a fair chance he'd be a GR member."

Jake wasn't interested in coincidences. That was over — it had actually happened, so it didn't matter now what the odds were.

"But there's more than three or four of them here, aren't there?" he said.

"That's what Jack was talking about when he said some of them hadn't recognized necessities. They planned this caper before the Epping Five got caught, so now he's had to pick members from outer groups, to do the Five's jobs. They had to have the right skills, you see, so he couldn't guarantee they'd be prepared to be as tough as he was."

"Mart, he did say you could tell us what they were doing."

"Yeah. Yeah. There's that. But what he says isn't the Propositions. They're themselves. He's ready to bust Prop Five, so you can't take his word on the others. Hell. I don't know what to do."

Jake said nothing. Granpa's breathing had changed. It was quick and shallow, as though he was finding it difficult to breathe, but he was still asleep.

"All right," whispered Martin suddenly. "I'l tell you. They're going to try and hijack an oil rig — one of the big, important ones. They'll let the crew go, and then they'll tell the government to let the Epping Five out of prison or they'll blow up the rig. They've got it all worked out. It isn't just the rig — though that's several million quid — it's the oil coming ashore and helping the balance of payments. They think they can set North Sea oil production back enough to matter."

Jake sighed. It was interesting. It was the reason why he was sitting with an aching head in this dank cavern. But knowing about it wasn't going to help much.

"Why've they only got three days?" he said.

"It's something to do with relief helicopters. There's a point in the routine when a big helicopter goes out with a dozen bods aboard. They've modified their own chopper to look like it. They've been monitoring the radio signals between the shore and the rig, and they've found a way to put the shore radio out of action. They've got their own transmitter on the yacht, and as soon as the shore radio goes phut they'll take over. If they time it dead right they ought to be able to get their own chopper down before anybody realizes what's happening."

"It sounds pretty complicated."

"Yeah. They'd worked it out in principle before the Five got caught. Their first idea was to hold the rig ransom in exchange for better pollution safeguards from the oil companies. Now they've brought it all forward to try and get the Five out."

"When they land on the rig they'll have guns?"

"Yeah. Jack told me that in a situation like that you've only got to fire a shot into the air and everybody does what you want. After what he said just now I don't know. Anyway, far as we're concerned, it's academic. We're stuck here. Oh, hell, Jake!"

Jake grunted sympathetically.

"They're right, you see," said Martin in a furious, hissing whisper. "They're right! GR is right! The Propositions are the only hope! Anything else, and by the time our kids are grown up the world will be spoiled! The whole world, and nothing will unspoil it. Time's running out, Jake."

Jake grunted again. His mind was fixed on a different scale of time. Three days. He didn't like the way Granpa's breathing kept changing.

"I wonder if there's a drier place further in," he said. "One of the side cells might do. I suppose we'd better move away from here in any case. Sergeant Abraham will come and look for us before three days, and if Mr. Andrews was telling the truth about the explosives . . ."

"No dice," said Martin sourly. "I told you I'd made a mess of things. You never asked me why Jack told me what they were up to. He didn't have to. I'd only assented as far as Prop Five. But he wanted to get me on his side. And I *was* on his side till I woke up and looked out of the window to see what the row was about and saw him hit you. But before that I'd rung up Sergeant Abraham — I couldn't get onto her because she'd gone home but I left a message with the desk sergeant — to say we were OK and we'd had an idea about some ghosts up on the Scotch border and we were going up there and we'd be in touch in two or three days' time. She won't come, Jake."

"Oh."

IN HIS DREAMS Jake remembered the ghost.

On the whole Jake didn't believe in ghosts. There were several reasons for this: he'd listened to Granpa's arguments since he was five; he'd three times joined Granpa on ghost hunts, and had not only thought but felt there wasn't anything there, no sad presences or tremors of old horrors — though one of the places had been a very spooky, echoing, creaking old vicarage near Petersfield; but mostly he didn't believe in ghosts for family reasons — when Granpa was away somebody had to stand up for him against Dad and Martin, so Jake had really argued himself into a position of sensible disbelief.

But that was the waking Jake. Dreams were different. In this dream he was running across a vast, shapeless, echoless upland, studded with tussocks of whippy grass which slashed his bare legs or tripped his feet. The ghost hunted him without pursuing him. Whichever way he ran it was there, creeping towards him, hooting. When he woke it was still there, faintly filling the dead air of the tunnel. It was all the life there was, the ghost of Annerton Pit. He forced himself wide awake, into the world of sensible disbelief.

His head was sore, but only on the outside. His left ear felt the wrong size. His whole body ached from the chill and damp of the tunnel and the discomfort of its floor. But the pain inside his head had faded. He remembered yesterday, the fear and shock and exhaustion. That had somehow faded too, leaving only worry and waiting. He wondered how long he'd slept. There was no way of telling, no morning traffic clatter or birdsong. He strained to listen to the sea, to guess where the tide had reached — it had been high just before they'd caught him, hadn't it? But the sound was too faint and his memory of it too imperfect to compare. He might, with practice, learn to tell the difference in a few days' time. A few days!

As he stopped listening for that particular sound the hoot came back, seeming to creep down the tunnel now. He spoke to drive it back.

"Is anyone awake?" he whispered.

"Haven't been asleep," said Martin aloud. "I couldn't stop thinking. Granpa, you're awake, aren't you? I wonder what the time is."

"Seven or eight," said Granpa. "How are you feeling, Jake?"

"Much better. Only stiff. My headache's gone. What about you?"

"A bit feverish. Is there anything to drink?"

In the ration sack were several cans, presumably from the hotel bar. You couldn't tell what you were getting till you opened one. Jake's was plain soda water. He ate half a dozen Garibaldi biscuits with it.

"Listen," burst out Martin. "Granpa, if I tell you what's up, will you promise not to tell anyone else, even the police, without my say-so?"

❖ 114

"Reluctantly," said Granpa, after a pause.

"Good enough," said Martin. "Well . . ."

"And situations could arise in which I felt I had to break my promise."

"OK," said Martin, who was now clearly just as determined to tell as the night before he'd been determined not to. The story was the same, only told more tidily, with fewer interruptions. When it was over Granpa said nothing.

"Well?" asked Martin angrily.

"They're like some people I knew once," said Granpa. "Africans — a really fine group, intelligent and brave, full of good ideas. That's how they started off. They finished up with half of them killing the other half and then terrorizing sixty villages — they called it liberating them — all in the name of those ideas."

"You're talking like a bloody racialist," said Martin.

"It isn't race — it's people. You could put your finger anywhere on a map of the world and find it had happened like that there, once. You could pick any date in history and find it was happening somewhere in the world then."

"Well, it isn't going to happen here, now!" shouted Martin. "If it wasn't for you two I'd go and kick that panel down and send up their whole explosives store. That'd bring the cops running, and Jack and his friends would never get to their famous rig. That's what makes me sick. They're going to get out there and somebody's going to get killed and that'll bring the whole GR movement into discredit. We've got a lot of people on our side now, or half on our side, because of the way we've done things. As soon as somebody gets killed we're going to lose the lot of them!"

The echoes of his anger died down the tunnel. Granpa groaned slightly as he shifted his position on his wuffling air mattress. The hoot, thin and vague though it was, seemed to fill the whole space. Jake began to fancy it was mocking him. There was only one way to drive it out of his mind, to exorcise the hooting ghost of his dream, and that was to find out what was making it. He stood up.

"All right if I explore?" he said.

"Good idea," said Martin. "See if you can find a dry bit. Yes, see if you can find somewhere which might be safe from a blast this end."

"No! Mart! You can't!"

"I'm not going to. Leave you two walled in? Don't worry, Jake. All right if he goes, Granpa?"

Granpa sighed, as though it was a nuisance to have to concentrate.

"I suppose so," he said. "If you think there's anything wrong with the air, Jake, have any trouble breathing, then back straight out. And put the empty cans under drips — you never know — we could be here more than three days."

Twenty yards up the tunnel Jake paused. He wished he had his stick. The floor was mostly smooth clay, slippery on the surface and slightly rubbery below, but here and there chunks of rock — or was it coal? — had fallen from the roof and were half embedded in the clay. He listened to the drips around him, tuning out the metallic tock of the can he'd placed under a more rapid drip a few yards back. He clicked his tongue against his palate to set up more echoes — yes, there was what Granpa had called a monks-working cell on his left, the third he'd passed, but the other two had been as drippy as the main tunnel. He moved to the entrance and clapped his hands. The echo came straight back of him, a curt denial, as though to say, "Not this way, buster." A couple of claps more and he knew that the chamber broadened from the entrance till it was about five feet wide and three or four times as long. It was empty, and felt no drier than anywhere else.

As he moved on up the tunnel he began to worry about Granpa's last words. If you have any trouble breathing . . . What had old Mr. Smith said about Annerton Pit? Never any trouble with gas. Never any explosions . . . But this wasn't Annerton Pit. Jake had done the Industrial Revolution in last year's history. He had never somehow got hold of it, and finished with poor marks, but he remembered strongly a description of the man dressed in layer on layer of damp rags who crawled round the mine with a flame on the end of a long stick, setting off little explosions in the pockets of gas that had built up near the roof, so they couldn't grow big enough to cause a real bang. There was chokedamp and firedamp. You had to keep the air moving. But the air in here was as still as the grave.

Close at hand the hill hooted. Now, *that* was moving air. And moving water too, rippling beneath the hoot. Jake moved more carefully forward, concentrating on the sound, tuning out the surrounding drips and echoes. Now more than ever it seemed to come out of the rocks all round him, until he was actually standing at what seemed to be its center, but still without being able to feel the slightest movement in the dead air of the mine.

He shrugged and was moving on when he realized that the nature of the floor had changed. It was as slimy as ever on the surface, but underneath was unyielding. A pace on and a pace back he found the familiar squidge of clay, but in the middle was this hard level patch. He stamped his foot on it, producing a thud that was barely a sound, more a resonance that traveled up the bones of his other leg. But yes, here the floor was hollow, and through the hollow place water was chuckling and air hooting. At the acid touch of reason the ghost melted into nothing.

Granpa and Martin were arguing as he came back, arguing about the ghost in Annerton Pit. It should have been reassuring to hear them, bringing back memories of similar arguments at home, but it wasn't. Granpa's voice was wrong, not the proper, dry, thoughtful, patient and vaguely amused tone which Jake was used to, but rapid, weak and fretful, a voice full of fever. Jake could hear that Martin wanted to stop, but Granpa wouldn't let him.

". . . looked up the records," Granpa was saying, "before I left Newcastle. It was a very wet spring and summer, just right for a rock slip, with the water table rising and lubricating strata that are normally dry. Both shafts blocked, cutting off ventilation. And, you see, the rock slip might release a big pocket of gas. Candles everywhere . . ."

"Hey," said Martin. "Davy had invented the safety lamp by then. That you, Jake?"

"Yes. Listen . . ."

"Hang on. Granpa's not going to rest till he's got this off his chest. Why no safety lamps, then?"

"Miners didn't like them," muttered Granpa. "Less light than candles. Even in fiery pits they'd try to get away with candles. So there was an explosion."

"Nobody heard one," said Martin, unable to prevent himself scoring the point, even though he must have known that Granpa had to get through the argument before he could rest.

"It could have been blanketed by the sound of the rock slip," said Granpa. "Or they didn't hear it at the surface through the blocked shafts. Or they did hear it and the owners suppressed the fact, because they hadn't been using safety lamps . . . after a big explosion you get a rush of chokedamp — carbon dioxide mixed with coal dust. They could all have been gathered at the bottom of the shaft and suffocated there, without a mark on them."

"They let it out of the rock," said Jake. He had dissolved his own ghost, but was still glad to help Granpa do the same to Mr. Smith's. "He meant the gas," he added.

"Yeah, what about him?" said Martin. "Mr. Smith's granny's uncle? What sent him off his chump then?"

"There are horrors enough in the real world," said Granpa, more calmly. "If you've been through a mine disaster you don't need ghosts. And one account I found called him a half-wit, which suggests that he may have been feebleminded before the accident. The explosion could have knocked him into a drainage shaft — miners call it an adit — and he'd have been washed out onto the beach more dead than alive. Did I say it had been a very wet year? There'd have been a good head of water — too much for the rescuers to work back against."

Now suddenly, he was sounding much more like his proper self, only rather tired and shaky. Martin laughed.

"Well, you got that off your chest, Granpa," he said. "Find anything, Jake?"

"I don't know. I didn't go right to the end. Everywhere's just as damp as everywhere else. There's one place where the floor's hollow. You can hear the wind hooting through, and water running."

"Wind?" said Martin. "That's got to come from somewhere. Are you sure?"

"Yes. I can hear it now. I don't expect you can. It was bothering me, so I went to look . . . What's the matter?"

"Banged my head getting up," said Martin. "Where are

you? Come on — let's go and see. Hey, where are you? Come and fetch me. Got you. You be all right, Granpa? Hey, this makes a change, doesn't it, Jake?"

Jake only grunted. He knew how Martin's sudden bursts of high spirits could flare up for a few minutes in the middle of trouble or depression and die away as fast as they'd come. Sometimes, when Jake had been much smaller, they'd played the game of turning out all the lights and letting Jake guide Martin round the house, but he didn't want to be reminded of that now. He led the way very carefully up the tunnel concentrating on drips and echoes.

A can, bashed into a rough trowel shape with a lump of rock, makes a feeble tool but it's better than nothing. At first Martin had wanted to make them a trowel each, but after five minutes' trial had agreed that it was better to work turn and turn about. The digging was easier for Jake — no different really from digging a hole in the garden at home. In fact the can was about as useful as the kind of tool a small child invents for itself. Only the floor of the tunnel wasn't good garden earth but packed clay which came away in small, greasy flakes. Every few minutes they had to work the can back into a better shape for digging.

Jake had felt the hard area above the hooting place with his fingertips and found that it was made of two large flagstones and a smaller one. They were now digging a trench three inches wide along the edge of this smaller one, hoping to be able to get their fingers under it and haul it up. Jake was hacking slivers of clay from the trench floor while Martin rested.

"Granpa's not too good," said Martin suddenly. "I got

him a drink while you were up the tunnel and I felt his forehead. He's running a real temperature."

"He sounded a bit better when we left," said Jake.

"Right. I think he goes up and down. When you were asleep he had almost a sort of fit, threshing about and sighing. He was quite compos — wouldn't let me do anything because he didn't want to wake you — then he eased off."

"Suppose this leads anywhere, what are you going to do?"

"I don't know. If you're right about water in there . . . You remember that bridge between the hotel and the sheds? That's over a little stream. I didn't actually look to see where it came from, but I've a sort of vague idea it came out of the cliff, about ten feet up. Judging by these flagstones it must be quite a big hole underneath — I mean they'd have just laid drainpipes otherwise — so with a bit of luck I might be able to get down there, crawl out, wait till it's dark, and climb the cliff."

With a bit of luck, thought Jake. It was all flimsy guesses, but already they were a solid structure in Martin's mind. Jake was digging hard — his hands were getting sore already from trying to grip and lever with the fragile, endlessly buckling tool — but he was doing so without much hope, simply because it was better than doing nothing.

"Then," said Martin, adding another story to his cardhouse, "I don't know. It was tough enough telling you and Granpa, but going to the cops and grassing on the whole GR movement . . ."

"Granpa's going to die," said Jake as flatly as he could.

"I know that! Oh, Jake, you get into something and you never guess how you're going to be forced to choose . . . Suppose I got out and went to the hotel. Suppose I managed to listen around for a bit and find out which of them were the soft ones, the ones Jack says don't recognize necessities. Suppose I could tell one or two of them about Granpa, and what Jack said about killing . . ."

Jake didn't say anything. He could tell from the tone that Martin knew this part of his building at least was fantasy. He concentrated on working the can along the edge of the flag, easing out a long slice of clay. When it came free it was like a small victory. With fingers part tender and part numb he felt into the trench to plan his next attack. An icy needle of air met his knuckles.

"We're getting somewhere," he said.

He had to duck to avoid a clash of skulls as Martin bent to feel.

"There," he said. "Got it?"

"Only just. Wait. Yes. Let's have that can. Damn. It isn't resting on earth. There's another stone or something underneath. I've bent the rotten can, too."

Jake hunkered round so that he could run his fingertips along the edge of the flagstone. It was rough cut, greasy with water like everything else, but with the texture of fine sandpaper beneath the grease. At its bottom edge he found a thin layer of crumbly stuff, and then, just above the new floor of the trench, another hard, straight-edged surface, but pocked and grainy.

"It's a brick, I think," he said. "The mortar's soft as soft."

"Let's feel. You're right. Ouch! What's a fingernail between friends? Anyway, we might be able to bash that brick in. I'll dig for a bit, Jake. You see if you can find a decent bashing stone."

As Jake rose he found that his neck and shoulders were a knotted network of aching tension, and the muscles of his forearms were taut with inner pressure. He put his hands in his pockets to try to draw a little warmth out of his thighs and prodded around the tunnel floor with his feet while Martin grunted and swore behind him.

Shifting the brick took an immeasurable time. They had to widen the trench in order to deepen it, and then scrape away at the damp mortar with little metal tabs from the drink cans. Most of the "stones" Jake found to bash with turned out to be soft coal, and the ones that were hard enough not to splinter at the first blow were shapes that made them even less useful as hammers than the can was as a trowel. The brick would move a sixteenth of an inch at one end. Bashing the other end would pivot the first end back to where it had been before. Then it would jam completely, and the boys would scrape feebly at the mortar that held it until the can tabs developed metal fatigue. By "lunchtime" they'd moved it half an inch. Granpa was very quiet while they ate. Jake felt his forehead and found it damp and chill, but Granpa twisted irritably away, muttering, "I'm all right, I tell you." Jake would have preferred to stay with him, but he had to guide Martin up the tunnel and once there he fell into the rhythm of bashing and scraping. Martin said very little, but worked with surprising persistence, as though the exhausting and painful task were a way of easing his anger and frustration. After a long while Jake went to see how Granpa was and found him in a restless doze. He was coming back up the tunnel, wondering how to persuade Martin that the digging wasn't worth the effort, when he heard the erratic thudding of stone on stone produce a different note.

"Done it!" muttered Martin.

"What?"

"You there, Jake? I think I've broken that vile brick."

"Hang on. Let me feel."

Martin was right. The surface of the brick was now a

pitted mess of chippings and clay and coal dust, but it ran in two distinct planes, one of which rocked when Jake pushed it. He picked up a stone and tapped carefully, nudging the half brick steadily further in. After a dozen taps it went with a rush. There was a rattle and a splash. The booming hoot below them, which by now Jake no longer noticed unless he listened for it, strengthened and changed. He felt the blast of wind and smelled the sea.

"Daylight!" whispered Martin.

And that was only a beginning. They had "tea" and told Granpa what they'd achieved, but though he understood he didn't seem very interested; instead, in a weak voice he insisted on repeating all his arguments about the Annerton Pit ghost. It was worrying and painful to listen to and Jake wished he'd stop, but Martin suddenly seized on a point.

"That might be it!" he said. "The drainage shaft Mr. Smith's granny's uncle got washed out through — we've found it."

"It's called an adit," insisted Granpa.

"All right, an adit. If he could get out that way, then I can! Come on, Jake!"

But they got barely further all that evening. The flagstone was immensely heavy, and jammed just as tight as the brick had been. Wearily Jake dug another trench along its opposite edge, while Martin scraped away at the clay that clogged the cracks between it and the neighboring stones. Martin levered out another brick without much trouble. He talked rather more between bouts of work, arguing to and fro over the question of what he ought to do when he got out. Instinctively they kept their voices down, as if their tenuous contact with the outside world might betray them to their enemies, though Jake was fairly sure that the noise of the sea and the wind would muffle any sounds they made. Suddenly Martin said, "Either my eyes are failing or it's getting dark. Let's give it one more heave and pack in."

Wearily Jake straightened. He'd been longing to stop for hours, but he wasn't used to giving in before Martin, and this time Martin seemed prepared to struggle on forever. They took their places on either side of the stone. Jake had to force himself to grip the harsh surface, his hand was so blistered; and it was slippery too with a mixture of clay and sweat and his own blood.

"We've been doing this wrong," said Martin. "We've got to break the suction. It's no use just heaving, we'll have to do it with a jerk. You heave as hard as you can and I'll do the jerking. Ready?"

Jake grunted and took the strain. It was like trying to lift the solid earth. He heard Martin hold his breath and then snort with sudden effort. A tremor ran through the stone.

"It's coming!" he whispered, and found somewhere a few pounds of extra strength. Martin snorted again, and this time the jar of his applied weight made more than a tremor.

"Hold it!" he gasped.

There was a brief, scrabbling noise.

"One, two, three, now!"

The slow buildup of fury and suppressed despair found its relief in an explosion of effort. The flag lifted an inch, coming with such suddenness that Jake lost his grip and tumbled backwards, gasping.

"You all right?" said Martin, panting. "Don't worry. I've wedged it with a stone. It'll come easy now, but I'm whacked. Let's give it a rest."

"I'm dead," said Jake.

They staggered back down the tunnel, found food, and

ate it without noticing what it was. It was difficult even to pay attention to Granpa, who had woken confused and rambling, and when Martin explained what they'd done simply said, "I leave it to you," in a vague old mumble. Jake didn't think he'd understood.

"OK," said Martin suddenly. "Back to work."

"No, Mart."

"Why not?"

"What are you going to do?"

"Finish getting that flag up. Crawl out. Climb the cliff."

"No, Mart. Listen. You're too tired. You won't make it. You've got to rest properly first. You'll fall. What are your hands like?"

"Sore as hell."

"You won't be able to hold on. Listen, Mart — let's have a bit of a rest. Granpa, tell him he's got to rest!"

Granpa answered in a language Jake didn't understand. Martin tried to laugh but it came out as a snort.

"All right," he said. "Supposing I can get out, it's too early to go anyway. I'll put a fresh can under that drip, and we'll go when it's full. You have a bit of a nap. I don't feel sleepy."

Jake stretched himself out on the groundsheet. No drips had fallen on it, but it was damp as if with the dew of the cave. Still, it was drier than the floor and he was too tired to notice its unyielding bumps and hollows. He heard Martin groping with the cans and began to count the metallic tock of the drops falling into the empty one. Before he was in double figures he was asleep.

I N HIS DREAM the hooting ghost returned. In a curious
way he knew where he was all the time he was asleep.
He was trapped in a tunnel next door to the main
Annerton Pit, where the ghost lived, and he and Martin
had opened a crack between the two mines, thus letting the
ghost come though. It chased them, hooting, down the tunnel. But at the same time the tunnel wasn't just a drift
mine; it was also the long, echoing corridors of school, and
the passages of Newcastle Police Station, and a hospital
where Granpa was waiting for a doctor who never came
while the blood dripped away from a wound in his wrist,
splash, splash, splash. Down all these windings and through
all these rooms Jake stumbled, looking for the doctor, with
the ghost sometimes hooting almost at his shoulder blades
and sometimes advancing at monstrous speed from the
furthest distance. All the time Granpa's life was dripping
away, splash, splash, splash.

He woke between one splash and the next. His hands
were puffy and sore. His clothes were dank. All his body
ached. The can was full. It had been full for some time,

splashing in his dream. Martin was sprawled beside him on the groundsheet, breathing slow and deep.

"Mart! Mart! Wake up!"

"Uh?"

"The can's full."

"Uh? What? Rotten sort of alarm clock. Uh? Lordie, but I needed that. You were dead right, Jake, not to let me go. How's Granpa?"

"I don't know."

"I can't hear him breathing!"

"I can. It's all right, Mart."

"He's got to last another day. He's got to! It isn't just because he's our grandfather, Jake. I'd feel just the same if I'd never met him in my life. They mustn't start not minding if people die. What's the point of busting yourself for peregrines and orchises if you stop worrying about people?"

They ate and went back to the flagstone. Stiffness and aches made Jake feel weak at first, and his hands winced from every touch, but he took off his socks and used them as gloves, and once they'd bullied their still sleep-drugged bodies into making the effort they found that the flagstone came up quite easily. The hoot changed its note as though they'd removed a stop from a giant musical instrument. The fresh, live sea air smelled like springtime. Martin knelt and craned through the gap.

"I can see a blob of light," he whispered. "It's still night, but it's not as dark as here. I'm going down. I wonder how deep that water is. Whee, it's icy. Hang on, Jake. I'm just going to take a look-see. I won't go without saying good-bye."

Once more the note of the moving air changed, becoming muffled and erratic as Martin twisted through the gap. The ripple of the water changed too, so that for a few yards

Jake could keep track of Martin's progress down the adit by the swirl of the stream around his feet. He waited, crouching by the hole in the tunnel floor, thinking, This is too good to be true. This is *King Solomon's Mines.* You're trapped deep underground, but of course there's a secret way out which you just happen to stumble on . . . He'd managed to suppress all hope by the time he heard the splash and ripple of Martin coming back up the adit. Something, even in those faint signals, told him that he'd been right.

"No good?" he said as Martin came slowly through the slot, all his tiredness back.

"How did you know? Never mind. Of all the foul luck!"

"What's up?"

"There's a sort of iron grating over the opening. Set into the rock. I don't think I can shift it."

"But Mr. Smith's granny's uncle got out."

"It's newer than that. Not dead new, but not a hundred years old either. They might have put it there to stop people climbing in — you know, when the hotel started or something — kids on holiday — you don't want them disappearing into old coal mines — of all the foul luck!"

He sat in silence, on the edge of tears. Jake knew it was better not to say anything for the moment, so he moved round the hole, knelt, and poked his head through. The water raced past about two feet below him. The adit seemed to be a little wider than that, a smooth shaft, circular in section and running dead straight into the hill. As far as he could reach it was lined with brick.

"Hell and hell again!" said Martin. "No point sitting here. Hell! No point in going back to Granpa either — I'm not going to sleep again tonight. You'd better try, Jake."

"I wonder what happens the other way," said Jake.

Even as he spoke a curious tremor ran through him. It

was as though the ghost, which so far had only haunted his dreams, had suddenly reached out an intangible tentacle and caressed his waking mind. If they were right — if this was the shaft down which Mr. Smith's granny's uncle had been washed — it led to Annerton Pit itself.

"Not much point going deeper in," said Martin. "Out is what we want."

"If the explosives blew up —" began Jake, then cut himself short. But it was too late.

"Hey, that's a thought! Even if it brought the cliff down it wouldn't matter. Somebody would come, and you could signal or shout from the grating!"

"No! Mart!"

Martin gave a sad chuckle.

"It's OK, Jake, I couldn't do it, not in cold blood. Actually walking up to the partition and kicking it in and blowing myself up. Suppose I'd been alone when I first thought of it . . . You know, I don't think I could have done it that way, either. Being angry isn't enough. You needn't worry, Jake."

A big load lifted. Consciously or subconsciously the idea had been nagging Jake's mind all the time, almost like his silly notions about the ghost that came and went so erratically.

"That's great," he said.

"How far does it go, d'you think?" said Martin.

"No idea. I can't hear beyond the hoot."

"Let's go, then. You up to it? Take off your shoes and socks and roll your trousers up. The water's icy, but it's only about six inches deep."

Jake led the way. Beyond the flagstones the shaft was circular in section and lined with brick, a bit under three feet wide and high. He had to move in a baboonlike crouch with his hands trailing in the bitter stream and his back rubbing the brick arch above. In a few yards he had no feeling in his feet at all. Their bodies muffled the flow of wind so that the hooting came now in wavering and gusty spasms, almost as though the hill were trying to make up its mind whether to swallow them or spit them out.

The stream swished and chuckled. The far shuffle and grunt of the sea dwindled until even Jake could no longer hear it. The shaft became a lifetime, endlessly reaching into the earth and never arriving. Its slope was very slight, only enough to make the water run down, but even so Jake began to feel that they'd climbed so far that they must soon come out into open air. The endless sameness of the journey, and the exhausting gait, and the cold all began to drug his mind and body, so that it took him a while to notice that something was different after all — there was a change in the soft, relentless hoot that had filled his hearing since first they'd climbed into the shaft. For a long time it had been all round him, shapeless and borderless; now it was behind, back, somewhere else, and he was outside it.

"We're getting somewhere," he said.

"Great. I thought I was going to spend the rest of my life doing this. Go careful, Jake — you don't know what this drains out of."

Jake crouched his way forward, feeling for footholds with his hands in the numbing water. Abruptly, in a very few yards, the floor of the shaft disappeared and at the same moment his head poked out into openness. He was still surrounded by rock but the new space seemed huge compared with the cramping shaft. When he clicked his tongue the echoes came sharply back from either side, but ahead of him they reached into distance. For a little way along that distance the water surface lay still, but further off it began to slither again. Water drips fell. A long way off something made a creaking groan. Jake froze at this new sound, shook his head, and clicked loudly back, listening and checking. Just beyond arm's reach to his right sheer rock rose from the dead surface of the water, but to his left the wall was several feet away, and between it and the shaft mouth was another surface, rising about two feet above the water. Bracing his right arm against the roof of the shaft to prevent himself toppling out into the pool he reached as far as he could to his left — yes, textureless under his numb fingers but perfectly solid was a wide shelf, the actual floor of the tunnel. The pool lay beside it, long and narrow. The mine drained into this pool and the shaft took the overflow out to the sea. Once more in the distance something groaned. He backed away down the shaft and explained what he'd found to Martin.

"Could you get out onto the shelf?" said Martin.

"Yes. Easy. Not so easy getting back, but I think I could do it. Do you want me to try?"

"No. Wait. We've got to think things out. Let's go back for Granpa."

"Mart, we'll never get him up here! He's much too ill."

"Uh-huh? He's lying on an inflatable rubber mattress. If we can get another of those flagstones up — I don't see why we shouldn't, now we can get our shoulders underneath — then we can drag him up the tunnel, lower him into the shaft, and just float him up here."

"What good'll that do?"

"I've been thinking. If we can get him out of the way, then we can walk the flagstones down the tunnel and I think I could use their weight to rig up a sort of deadfall. You can unravel the food sack for me. That'll give me enough cord —"

"It won't be very strong."

"It won't have to be. The stones will be balanced. It'll only need a touch to topple them. If I've got enough cord to get right away up the tunnel into one of those cells, then I can topple the stones against the partition and set the explosives off . . ."

"It sounds hellish dangerous, Mart. And complicated."

"Yeah. Two to one it won't work. If it doesn't, then we'll have to explore further, see where this air current goes to, see if I can get out that way."

"Why not do that now, Mart? Leave Granpa where he is and —"

"Because I've got to give the other thing a try. If we can set the explosives off, then the whole oil-rig caper will be off. They won't be able to do it. They'll pack it in. But if I go and get the cops while they're still setting up the oil-rig caper, then they'll get charged with that. It'll be almost as bad for GR as if they'd brought it off. Sorry, Jake . . ."

"But Granpa —"

"Look, even supposing there's a way out, I'd be lucky to make it before daylight. Then there's every chance they'd spot me. So there's no point in starting till after dark, anyway. Give me till then to try and set this other thing up. We can tell when by looking out the other end of the shaft. Please, Jake."

Jake said nothing. While they'd been arguing he'd forgotten about the cramping shaft and the icy stream. He thought Martin was wrong, though he didn't understand about the deadfall, but Martin was good at that sort of thing. If Martin said it might work, then it might. Even so, it was obviously better sense to go on, to try and find a way out now. There must be one for the wind to blow so steadily up the shaft. But he didn't go on arguing, partly because he thought he wouldn't win, but partly because he was afraid — afraid of the whispering, groaning maze of tunnels beyond the pool. Annerton Pit itself. He would rather go back than face that now, so he gave in.

Martin said nothing on the way down until they reached the slot they had made into the drift mine. They were standing in the tunnel, enjoying the feel of straightening out hunched backs and cramped limbs, when he laughed.

"I've realized something about GR," he said. "About life, I suppose. It's not much of a problem *being* right. It's *doing* right where the trouble begins — doing it and going on doing it while life comes up and hits you with situations where there aren't any rights to do. Feel like lifting this flag? We'll do it from this end. I'll get under it and you stay up there. Right?"

To Jake's astonishment it took them about a minute, though the stone must have been twice as heavy as the earlier one. They propped it against the tunnel wall and went to find Granpa. He was awake and in his right mind, though he couldn't speak above a whisper. Martin explained his ideas.

"If you must you must," said Granpa. "You'll need to be at least forty yards away, lying flat on the floor in one of the cells. And there's a good chance you'll bring the roof down, even there. But provided you can get Jake clear . . ."

"Then it's my funeral," said Martin, very cheerfully. "Now let's see about packing you up. We'll drag you up on the groundsheet so that we don't puncture the mattress . . ."

That part of the plan went easily too. They were maneuvering to lower Granpa and the mattress into the drainage shaft when Martin said, "Hello, it's getting light. Good. I'll be able to do some of the work up here, see what knots I'm tying. Ready, Granpa?"

The actual lowering was tricky, but didn't take long. The journey up the shaft was torture. Jake shuffled along backwards, huddled and icy, with his fingers hooked through the two brass rings let in to the corners of the inflatable pillow. Martin pushed behind. Every twenty yards or so they had to rest, but resting in that position was almost as painful as moving, and seemed to let the chill of the stream soak deeper into the body. Then movement brought no warmth back, but only reminded the body how tired it was. The bruise on the side of Jake's face, which so far he'd mostly forgotten about, began to wince with fresh aches. He lost himself in the endless ritual of rest and shuffle, rest and shuffle. The water swished round the mattress and the wind whimpered as if it were complaining of the way their bodies blocked its flow.

Jake was resting when he realized that they'd at last reached the end. He knew before he noticed that the wind noise had changed. As soon as he consciously listened he could hear the difference, but before that he had been aware of something else — the sense of narrowness ending, the wider space beyond, and in that space something waiting.

"On we go, Jake. Can't be much further now."

"It isn't. I can hear the end."

"Great. It's beginning to give me the creeps, this hole."

The something didn't seem to move or react as Jake, swallowing hard, backed painfully up towards it. At the end of the shaft he stopped, twisted round, swallowed again, and clicked his tongue. The noise floated out over the pool, meeting no new obstacles. At the same instant the something seemed to withdraw, to vanish without one tremor of movement into the dripping galleries beyond. It was here, down in this dark maze, that the miners and their wives and children had rushed and huddled. For a moment Jake knew the same panic. He almost turned back down the shaft, but the thought of Granpa stopped him. What could he say to Granpa? At the same instant another thought came to him. The miners had been used to the dark, but even so they had been sighted people — used to the dark but used too to the prick of light at the end of a gallery where candles shone, to the approaching glow of a lamp carried by a comrade. If Granpa was right and there'd been an explosion, that would have blown out all the candles and they would have been afraid to light another for fear of more explosions. They'd have been in total dark, where the mind breeds its own terrors.

"It isn't dark for me," Jake muttered.

He moved at once, giving his own mind no time to hesitate again. Crouching at the mouth of the shaft he reached out with his left hand and as soon as it touched the shelf which was the main tunnel floor he threw his weight onto that arm and brought his right arm over beside it. He stayed poised for an instant, bridged over the pool, then bent his knees and jumped up and sideways in a gawky half-vault. His left leg dragged in the water but it was already soaked from the stream in the shaft. His right knee found the ledge. Done it!

"All right," he said, lying down and reaching out across the pool to feel for the mattress as Martin floated it clear. Nothing happened. Martin was muttering to himself — swearing quietly. Jake realized that he too was recovering from a sudden wave of fright.

"Come on, Mart. It's OK. I'm ready."

Deliberately he spoke in a louder voice. The gallery beyond him echoed, "Ready, ready, ready." Martin stopped swearing. The mattress floated smoothly out into the pool, so that Jake, tugging at one corner, could drift it up alongside the shelf he was on. He pulled it well clear, went back, found Martin's groping hand, and helped him to cross the gap. At last they stood panting side by side.

"What a place!" whispered Martin. "What a place!"

Jake could hear the shudder in his voice but knew that he wasn't going to admit that he'd been on the edge of panic. Jake didn't want to say anything either — he didn't like the idea of his imagination playing tricks on him like that. It was over now. The world was real and sensible again. Even the hoot in the shaft seemed reassuring, steadied to its normal note now that their bodies were out of its path.

"How are we going to get Granpa up here?" said Martin. "It's too far to lift."

"Let's try the far end. The water isn't falling in, it's more sort of slithering," said Jake.

He walked up beside the pool and found that it ran for almost twenty yards. Halfway along it a side gallery opened on the left and a thin smear of water ran across the ledge and trickled into the pool, but at the far end a much larger stream, as big as the flow in the drainage shaft, rustled down a shallow slope to the water.

"It's all right," he called. "We can drag him out here."

Behind him, loud as a voice at his shoulder, the echo answered, "Here. Here. Here."

Ten minutes later Jake was sitting on a pile of coal at the entrance to the side gallery trying to think himself warm. Granpa lay on the floor beside him breathing so faintly that Jake could barely hear him. Martin was further along, leaning against the wall while he massaged his own legs, and muttering under his breath, still occasionally caught in the backwash of the retreating wave of terror.

Jake kept telling himself that he'd got over that. It had been a product of his own shock and tiredness, and possibly too he'd picked up a feeling from Martin — that'd explain their shared fright — and Martin had every right to be frightened of what he was going to have to do down in the drift mine. There'd been nothing there — only Jake's own fear. Anything else was nonsense.

And yet he couldn't help listening with pricked ears to the noises of this place as though a real monster stalked its galleries. Far off in various distances he could trace the rustle and pattering of water. The stream slithered in at one end of the pool and out at the other. The wind in the shaft hooted steadily. Then, loud and near, came the creaking groan he'd heard before. His nape prickled and his breathing stopped.

"What the hell's that?" whispered Martin.

"Timber," muttered Granpa. "Old pitprop. Nothing. Nothing."

"Glad to hear it," said Martin. "Right. Back to work, all. Jake, I'll need you for a bit, if you can face it."

"OK."

"Right. You go first. I'll anchor you here while you find the hole. Where are you? Got you. Right."

Leaning across the pool Jake found the curve of brickwork that marked the mouth of the shaft. He focused his hearing on the ripple of water, trying to judge the swing of his leg to bring his foot down at the point where it left the pool. The moan of wind in the shaft wavered, almost died, rose again and dwindled. Jake froze on the brink of movement.

"There's someone in the shaft," he whispered.

"Can't be."

"Listen."

Now he was sure of it. When he'd been in the middle of the shaft the wavering and whimpering had sounded different because it was all round him, but he knew it was the same effect.

"Hell!" said Martin. "Oh, hell!"

"They're quite a long way down," said Jake. "We might be able to find the way out. This air must go somewhere."

"They'll have torches," said Martin. "They'll be able to move quicker than us — quicker than you, even, Jake. And if we're dragging Granpa."

"You leave me here," whispered Granpa. "I won't last long, in any case. I'm pretty well done for."

"No you're not!" snapped Martin. "Jake, look, they've still got to get out of that hole and cross the pool. They can't fight while they're doing that. They've got to come one at a time. If you could find something to chuck at them . . ."

"I was sitting on a pile of coal. There were some pretty hefty bits."

"That'll do. A dozen good lumps, at least."

Choosing the pieces of coal and ferrying them to where Martin waited tensely by the mouth of the shaft, Jake didn't pause to think what they'd do, supposing they won this skirmish. His mind was filled with a pounding fury, a lust to lash out, to wound and kill, to show these people that if they hurt him they'd get hurt back. Supposing Martin got in a good shot with his first lump it might lay the leading man out — he'd fall into the pool and drown. Jake thought eagerly about this. His fingers caressed the jaggedness of the chunk of coal he was carrying.

"If they've got torches," he whispered, "you'll be able to see to aim."

"Right. How near are they?"

"Long way still. They're probably checking the grating at the bottom. I won't know till I hear the water noise change. The wind noise is too difficult."

"OK. Fetch us a few more missiles. I'll probably see their torches first."

It was a long time before that happened. Jake found more than twenty good pieces of coal and arranged them against the end wall of the gallery where he could pick them up without fumbling. He was crouched beside them, shivering with tension, when Martin whispered, "There's a light coming . . . no . . . yes . . ."

Jake strained to listen. Yes, the stream had changed its sound and was lisping past obstacles that came and went. He heard a distinct splash and the mutter of a voice. He found his jaw was aching from the force with which he'd been clenching his teeth. Martin was breathing in slow, deep gulps, as if he was in a trance. A voice, hollow with the resonance of the shaft, said, "We're getting to the end. Hang on." The sound of the stream steadied, rustling past an obstacle only a foot or two from the pool.

"Hang on," said the man — it was the one Jake thought of as the schoolmaster. "Deep water. I thought you said the old boy was too groggy for this sort of thing."

"Get on," said the muffled voice of the man behind. "See what's round the corner."

The ripple changed. Martin's arms swooshed down. The man's grunt of surprise became a yell of pain choked off in a splash. There was a rattle and a different yell inside the shaft. Jake found he was screaming in a strange, harsh voice like a parrot's, "Kill 'em! Kill 'em!" The yells and thuds and screams came moaning and whining back from the echoing depths of the mine. When Jake tried to pass Martin a fresh lump he found he must have thrown the one he was holding ready — and only then he remembered his round-arm swing at the mouth of the shaft. A ricochet off the brickwork must have caught the second man hard enough to make him yell. As the echoes died there came a soft, threshing noise where the stream ran into the shaft. Martin was still breathing with dreamlike slowness as he bent to scrabble up another lump of coal. He stood upright, paused an instant, and grunted with effort as his arms swooshed down. This time there was no yell, only a thud and splash.

"Oi! Stop that! You'll kill him!" shouted the second man.

Jake had a fresh lump ready but Martin twisted the other way to find one for himself. Before he was upright again Jake heard a sloppy, dragging sound in the mouth of the shaft. Once more the stream changed its ripple, as though an obstruction had been pulled away.

"Hold my arm," said Martin. "Stop me falling in."

He found Jake's hand without hesitation. Jake took the strain, leaning away from the pool. Martin's free arm swished through the air. At almost the same moment came another thud and yell from the shaft, followed by more dragging sounds, dwindling as the man hauled his unconscious comrade out of range. Suddenly Martin laughed. The wild sound echoed among the tunnels like the cry of a hunting beast. He picked up another lump, leaned out again over the pool, and swung. This time there was no more than a rattle and a splash. Jake realized that he'd been moving with sudden certainty.

"They're too far down, Mart. Can you see?"

"He dropped his torch in the pool. It's one of those waterproof ones and it's still shining down there. I can see just a bit. I laid him out, Jake . . . I may have killed him . . . You know, I wanted to kill him . . . I never thought . . ."

Martin took one more long, deep gasp and let it go as a sobbing sigh. Jake, too, felt the tension going. His throat was sore with shouting. He was very tired. It was an effort to force himself to listen to the noises in the shaft. Murmur of voices, one asking a question, the other gasping an answer.

"It's all right," whispered Jake. "He's alive. I can hear them talking."

"Thank God!"

"Hold it! He's coming back. He's moving carefully."

"Hell! All right, if that's the way they want it . . ."

They took up their positions again. Jake's prickling awareness reached out into all the maze of the mine. He tried to concentrate on the small sounds in the shaft, but the drips and creakings in the galleries kept snagging at his mind. They seemed to come nearer and then retreat in slow pulses, as though they were sounds set up by the movement of a live creature, like the erratic crackle of dry leaves made by a predator stalking through undergrowth. The man in the shaft, carefully though he was moving, couldn't prevent the stream rippling around his feet. The ripples came nearer. They were close. Jake touched Martin's knee and pointed to the shaft. He heard Martin's arms rise above his head, but this time his breathing was normal. The man paused just inside the mouth of the shaft. Jake could hear no change in the noise of the water, but all at once Martin's arms whooshed down. There was a light, puffing sound blotted out by a splash. Martin grabbed at the lump of coal Jake held ready and as he threw it an appalling clamor filled the galleries, numbing Jake's hearing for several seconds. Then Martin was shouting, sour and angry.

". . . keep this up all day if you want!"

More echoes.

"He'll have the roof down," whispered Granpa as they died.

"You hear that, Dave?" snapped Martin. "You fire your gun again and you'll have the roof down."

"Come off it," said Dave.

"You come off it. My grandfather's a mining engineer. He knows what he's talking about. That brickwork in there's a hundred years old and the mortar's soft as bread. You want it down on you, and the water piling up, and you drowning underneath?"

Silence.

"What happened?" whispered Jake.

"He rolled up his jersey or something," muttered Martin. "Made me think it was his head. Took a shot at me before I'd got something else to chuck. He won't catch me like that again."

They waited in aching tautness. Slowly Jake began to feel that they were not alone, that somewhere close by in one of the galleries a presence had appeared and was waiting . . . Angrily he shook his head. He'd been through all this. When you're tired and frightened your mind plays tricks on you. That was all.

As if to prove it the imagined horror vanished at the sound of Dave's voice.

"All right," he said, speaking quietly and quickly. "If that's the way you want it. You've caused enough trouble already, and I've got better things to do than to sit here arguing. You can stay here or come down after me. It's up to you. You've got half an hour to make up your minds. If you aren't out by then I'm going to block this tunnel. The water'll pile up, like you say, and you'll be the wrong side of it. You think anyone'll come and look for you up here? Not bloody likely. Got it? Half an hour. So long."

He seemed almost to scuttle away down the stream. The

movement made Jake realize something that he hadn't noticed while he'd been absorbing the actual meaning of Dave's threat. On the surface Dave's voice had been in key with that meaning, impatient, angry, decisive. But underneath had been something else. Dave had been frightened. Not frightened of Martin's missiles — with a little more effort he could surely have forced his way out of the shaft and onto the ledge where they huddled.

But he hadn't, because he'd been frightened of Annerton Pit.

IO

"HALF AN HOUR," said Martin. "We'd better get
going."
"Where?"
"See if we can find where this wind goes out. How far
will it be, Granpa?"
"I don't know," whispered Granpa. "Not too far. Not a
big mine."
"Dave may be bluffing, but I'm not risking anything on
that. Say ten minutes there. See if it's any use. Ten min-
utes back if it isn't. That gives us ten minutes to get back
down the shaft before he blocks it. We'll be going with the
stream. OK?"
"What about the torch?"
Martin hesitated.
"Too deep," he said. "I don't think I can make it. You
can take me, Jake. That's just as good."
"OK. Give me your hand."
"Fast as you can go. So long, Granpa."
The gallery was lower and narrower than the drift mine
had been. Martin had to stoop, and Jake was constantly

aware of the roughhewn roof only an inch or two above his head. The floor was treacherous — there seemed to be a series of ridges across it, sometimes squishy but sometimes hard enough to trip over. Martin kept stumbling. Galleries opened to right and left at much more regular intervals than in the drift mine, and at some of these entrances the air current swirled and flapped, but mostly it drove steadily on. The tunnel shaped itself ahead in drips and the rustle of the stream and the echoes of their own stumbling footsteps. Hurry drove out fear, except that once or twice Jake had to make an effort of will to ease his grip on Martin's hand. If it hadn't been for the ridges —

Martin caught his foot and fell sprawling.

"These damn things," he muttered. "You'd have thought they'd have had the sense to make the floor level."

Jake hadn't thought at all. He'd just accepted the mine as it was, an obstacle to be got through. But now Martin had made the point he noticed that the ridge he was standing on was firmer than most and flat-topped. He probed sideways with his shoe and found a soft line of something — rotten wood, by the feel, running at right angles to the ridges along the floor of the tunnel.

"They're sleepers," he said. "There must have been a railway track along here, one with wooden rails."

"Right," said Martin. "Let's try taking longer steps. What's that noise?"

"Falling water, I think. But there's something else first."

They moved on more smoothly, now that they'd found that the sleepers were regularly spaced, but in another thirty yards Jake almost tripped over a sudden soft obstruction. He'd been pacing automatically from sleeper to sleeper, concentrating on the area ahead where the air current audibly moved in a muddled way, and the small echoes came back as if from a blank wall.

"Hold it." he said. "We've reached a sort of junction. Left or right?"

He realized that they had come up the leg of a T, whose arms now stretched to either side. From both directions he could hear the ripple of a drainage stream, but from the right this was confused by the splash of falling water. What he'd tripped over was the point of the crossing rail tracks.

"Left," said Martin. "The other way sounds a bit wet."

"OK."

A stumble or two among the irregular sleepers of the junction, and Jake could move forward again at a smooth pace. Everything was just the same as in the other tunnel — the stream, the drips, the creaking echoes, the guiding air current — but it felt quite different. Suddenly it was harder to take the full pace from one sleeper to the next, and Martin's grip on Jake's hand was so tight that it hurt.

"This doesn't feel right," muttered Martin.

"The wind's not so strong," whispered Jake.

"Let's try the other way."

"OK."

They turned back into the wind, but the intangible pressure behind them seemed stronger, blowing them through the muddle of the junction and on into the tunnel beyond.

"That's more like it," said Martin in a normal voice.

Jake grunted. Consciously he was aware that the air current was no stronger in this arm of the galleries, but still it seemed easier to follow. Ten minutes, he thought. How long have we had? Four minutes? Five? The noise of falling water grew steadily nearer, a thin stream tumbling from a height, like a cistern overflowing from an upper story into a street below. The sound set up a mess of echoes, but among them Jake was aware of a low mass blocking the gallery almost from side to side. He slowed, clicked his tongue, and stretched out his free hand. Three more paces brought him into touch with what at first seemed just a pile of coal, only too high for its width. He moved his hand and found that the stuff was heaped into a square-sided wooden container, about three feet wide — a little truck — no, a whole line of trucks. He nudged with a foot and found a small iron wheel which had pressed right through the rotted rail below.

"Trucks," he said. "We'll have to squeeze past. It sounds like there's a blank wall beyond."

"The air's still blowing."

Jake stood still and tried to tune out the water noises. He could just hear the faint rub of wind passing a narrow place, quite high.

"We're going to have to climb," he said. "You can't see daylight or anything?"

"Nowt. This doesn't look too good, Jake."

"Let's give it a try."

Edging up beside the trucks Jake found that the gallery widened as if to make room for miners to work alongside them. He was beginning to stride forward when his shin banged into a hard bar.

"Hold on," he said. "There's something here. It might be a ladder. Yes. Iron rungs. They go into the rock on that side. It's a big wooden beam this side . . ."

He clutched gingerly at the timber. It was slimy with the spray of the tumbling water and as he grasped it more water oozed out between his fingers, like juice from a squeezed orange.

"The wood's dead rotten," he said. "I'll try the first rung."

The rusted iron was stout and round at each end, but in the middle it was bowed down and flattened on top, worn and bent to that shape by the endless climbing of miners, children no older than Jake, very likely, carrying their own weight of coal in baskets on their backs. Jake trod right at the wall end of each rung, counting as he climbed. The fourth was loose and the soggy timber barely held it in place. The ninth was missing and the last three were loose like the third. There were sixteen in all. At the top Jake found the rotted remains of a large trapdoor through which the updraft funneled. It opened into yet another gallery with its rustling drainage stream, the water of which fell to the floor below. This gallery sounded lower and narrower than the one they'd been in. Somewhere along it a different movement of wind made a steady, dull snore.

"I'm up," he called. "It's all right if you put your weight close to the wall. I'll tell you which rungs are dicey."

Martin came steadily up, counting the rungs as he climbed. At the twelfth rung he stopped.

"Where are you?" he said.

Jake leaned over the edge of the trapdoor.

"Click your fingers," he said. "There. Got you."

Perhaps Jake's touch made Martin careless, or perhaps Martin's extra weight made the difference, but he'd climbed one more rung when there was a soft, tearing noise. Jake was jerked harshly forward. Iron clashed and tinkled. For a moment Jake thought he was going to be pulled through the trapdoor, but Martin must have had some other handhold. He stopped falling when he'd seemed almost gone.

"Let go," he gasped.

Jake did so. He heard that hand scrabble for a grip. Martin grunted with effort and seemed to flow up through the hole in one smooth rush and collapse panting, half across Jake's body.

"Nasty," he said. "First prize for gymnastics, though. Whew. You OK?"

"I think so. What happened to the ladder?"

"Gave completely. We'll have to go on, now. Ready when you are."

Now Jake had to move at a half crouch, with his right arm checking the tunnel wall and his left stretched achingly in front of him to feel for projections from the low roof. Martin came behind with his hand on Jake's shoulder. There was no rail track, so the floor was easier. The windy snore came nearer, too steady a note to be what Jake had been hoping for, the thresh and gust of the true wind sweeping the outer world. The stream suddenly disappeared, flowing out of one of the blind galleries on their right and leaving only a slimy smear of gathered drops along the floor ahead. Springs in the depths of the hills must feed these drainage streams, Jake thought. The tunneling miners let them out of the rock . . .

He scuttled on, dragging Martin behind him. His senses, particularly his hearing, seemed to have grown beyond the frontier of his skin, forming a sensitive shell of awareness outside his body, so that he knew the shapes and natures of the things around him without having to stop and think. Where rocks had fallen from the roof he avoided them almost unaware of what he was doing. The wind seemed to be blowing him along the tunnel like a dry leaf. The snoring noise ahead came nearer, but before they reached it he knew what it was — the miners had dug their tunnels to make a circle; down below the air current had split, going along both arms of the circle; here it was joining up again to make its escape.

As they reached the place he paused. The dusty draft buffeted in from the left. It was only wind, and beyond it — not far on now, surely — must be the place where it rose to the outer air. The by-pit, Mr. Smith had called it. Where the men on the surface had dug their way down to fetch out the bodies of the dead miners. It was only wind, but it seemed like an obstacle.

"What's up?" said Martin. "Hey! I can see! I had my eyes shut because of the dust. Why didn't you tell me? Come on!"

He pushed past, dragging Jake through the mess of eddying air and on, while the wind, doubled in strength now, swirled them along. Ahead of him Martin stumbled and grunted.

"Look out, Jake. Rockfall."

"I thought you could see."

"Just a patch of light. Hang on. The whole roof's given here. Look out for falling bits . . ."

A dislodged stone rattled down a slope of rock. Martin's voice moved upward. Jake, probing carefully behind, nudged his foot against a boulder, got to his knees, and began to crawl up a steep slope of scree. Behind him the air current made its snoring noise where the two tunnels joined, but ahead he could now hear the sound his ears had so long been pricked for, the swish and scurry of the sea wind as it threshed among branches. As the rock pile rose so did the roof, but not so sharply, so that the space into which he was climbing steadily narrowed. Ahead of him Martin wriggled and scrabbled, panting more with excitement than with effort. Suddenly these noises stopped.

"So far, so good," said Martin in a meditative voice.

"Can you see out? How far is it?"

"I don't know. Fifty foot? There's bushes or something at the top. I expect they planted a thorn hedge round it, stop sheep falling down, and it's become a thicket. Umm. It's not going to be that easy, Jake. Let's see . . ."

"Don't try it if —"

"I've got to, haven't I? Don't be stupid. I can't get this far without giving it a go. The top half looks fairly possible — they've lined it with something — timber I think — and there's ribs every so often. Provided they haven't rotted. Hang on, that looks like a rung. Yes, and . . . There's iron rungs up there, let into the side. If I could make it to there . . . trouble is, down here it's all overhang where the shaft caved in . . ."

By this time Jake was crawling upward through a slot where the jagged rock of the roof touched his back. The air current squeezed through the slot, plucking at his anorak and trousers in its rush to the outer world. The crannies between the rocks he was climbing were soft with fallen litter, leaves and twigs that had rotted to fine mold.

He rose to his feet and stood beside Martin at the top of the cone of fallen rock. The air current picked out the space around him, another cone, more sharply pointed, narrowing at the top to a shaft up which the air made its final swishing rush.

Martin was still muttering to himself in the vague, almost scholarly manner he used when he was tackling a job he thoroughly understood.

"That's the only possible . . . umm . . . if that's not loose . . . might do, provided . . . umm. Right, move over a bit, Jake."

Jake shifted. He heard a grunt and crash, followed by the slither of smaller stones down the slope. Scrapings, clicks and mutters as Martin piled more stones. Time passed. They weren't going to make it back, not in the half hour . . .

"Now, you come and stand here," said Martin. "I've made a bit of a cairn. I'll need you to steady me while I stand on it, and then I might have to put a foot on your shoulder, so be ready for that. Right?"

Jake did as he was told, stood, steadied, waited, took the sudden thrust of Martin's foot, got both hands under it and heaved upwards just as his knees began to buckle with the weight. He lost his balance and fell slithering on the rough rock. Small stones pattered round him.

"Great," gasped Martin. "Better move out from there, in case anything big comes down. That includes me. Now . . ."

Aching from the fall Jake crawled back through the slit between the roof and the rock pile and waited, listening. Martin climbed on, encouraging himself with mutters before each fresh effort. Once he let out a shout of surprise and a whole hail of stone rattled down. There was a long pause, then he began to mutter again. The sounds moved slowly further away. Jake sat in the nagging draft obsessed with exhaustion and loneliness. His body was full of pains, hands still sore from digging, head aching and puffy with its bruise, a different ache in his hip whose cause he couldn't remember, and all the wincing little stiffnesses of joints and muscles that he had used to their limit and then rested on the hard earth of this chill, dank underworld.

"Jake," called Martin's voice softly above him.

"Uh-huh?"

"I've got to the lining. I'm pretty sure I can make it from here. The wood's rotten but the hoops are iron. Listen, I'm going to try and go quietly in case they've got someone watching. I'll cuckoo if it's all clear. Right?"

"OK. Good luck."

"Same to you."

The noises of climbing were smaller now and steadier, and moved more quickly away. Fragments still fell, but with soft paffing noises that told Jake they were things like flakes of rusted iron or splinters of rotten wood or fallen leaves dislodged from ledges. But as these sounds dwindled the noises of the mine began to seem louder again. Previously the snore of the two air currents meeting had blanketed most of them off, but now that he was used to it he could sense again the whispering maze beyond. Jake thought of the old miners who had hacked out all these galleries, and their children hauling the coal away, bent double under loaded baskets, as tired as Jake felt now, as sore and aching, day after day, shift after shift . . .

A cuckoo called once, twice. He answered it, then twisted from his crouch and half crawled, half slithered down to the old floor of the tunnel. He didn't think of staying where he was. The important thing was to get back to Granpa — not to leave him alone, ill, dying perhaps, in Annerton Pit. The draft still snored monotonously into the tunnel and swished to freedom up the shaft. They must have taken more than half an hour, Jake thought — ten minutes — no, nearly twice that — to reach this place and longer still for Martin to climb out. So Dave had been bluffing. Or he'd come back . . .

Jake walked rapidly down the tunnel to the opening where the other draft bucketed in from the right and without hesitation turned into it. His sense of urgency drowned out the vague feelings of reluctance he'd had about facing this arm of the circuit. Because of the broken ladder he couldn't go back the way they'd come, so this was the only chance. But it was new territory. Suppose Dave hadn't been bluffing, but had been delayed, or was allowing them a bit more rope; then when he blocked the drainage shaft the air current would die and it would be much harder for Jake to find his way. And at the same time the water would rise in the pool and cover the tunnel floor and go on rising. Granpa's mattress would float, but how would Jake reach him? And if Granpa had another of his bouts of fever and started threshing about . . .

As fast as his sore hip allowed Jake limped along with the dusty wind in his face. There was nothing to show that this new gallery was different from the one he had turned out of. It was narrow and low roofed, with the same slimy floor, the same drips and creaks and echoes, and the same side galleries making sudden changes in the resonance of its walls. The slime gathered and became a sloppy trickle. A spring-fed stream runneled out from the right and joined this to make a whispering flow. That must finish up in the pool, Jake thought. If they block the air current I'll be able to follow that. It must be almost half an hour. Perhaps Dave has come back. I wasn't there to listen for them. They've got Granpa. They're stalking me through the mine . . .

The thought didn't make him slow his pace; he hurried on, straining more carefully for sounds that didn't belong in the pit. There was another obstruction ahead, a place where the tunnel narrowed and the wind came breathily through. He slowed as he approached it, reaching for the tangible edge of the draft until his hand touched wood, greasy and soft with decay, but with ridges like plowland where the harder line of each year's grain had resisted the rots. His thumb touched a rusted hinge. The remains of a door dangled half open . . . Suddenly his mind spat up another little fragment of the Industrial Revolution — a child sitting hour after hour in the dripping dark by just such a door as this, opening it to let the miners through, shutting it behind them, opening, shutting, waiting, opening, shutting, waiting — so that the precious air currents should be forced to scour through all the windings of the mine. There had to be two air shafts of course — you couldn't rely on the drainage shaft not being full of water sometimes. Behind Jake lay the by-pit where Martin had climbed up — that was to let the stale air out. Ahead some-

155 ❖

where lay the main shaft which had let the fresh air in. But that was blocked now, blocked for a hundred and forty years, and at its foot a whole shift of miners, men, women and children, had died.

The thought made Jake pause. Then with a little reluctant grunt he stepped through the door.

11

THE CHANGE came gradually, like the unnoticed onset of sleep, or like mist which has no tangible water drops in it but which you find has somehow soaked you through. Jake must have gone twenty paces before he realized that he was no longer hurrying, that he was moving with short, groping steps, that he had stopped listening properly to the mine noises around him, and his senses had shrunk back to himself, that he was afraid. A vague fear, not of Dave, nor even of the dead miners — though it seemed to have begun with them. It was like stories of the purring growl of tigers which seems to come from every direction, so that a terrified traveler will suddenly panic and rush into the claws of the waiting monster. Jake stood still, but the vague noises of the mine seemed now to be closing in on him. It's coming, he thought.

"It's coming," whispered the empty gallery beside him. His own lips must have spoken the words, though he couldn't remember moving them. With a spasm of will he clapped his palms together. The wince of their soreness seemed to clear his mind just as the echoes of the clap cleared the stretching galleries. There was nothing near him, either before or behind, but as the echoes faded the muffling, almost furry gas of fear closed round him again. He could hear the mine noises only if he actually listened to them. It's dark, he thought. This is how sighted people feel in the dark . . .

"It isn't dark for me."

"Dark for me."

He clapped his hands again and while the sound was still probing the galleries, limped on, leaning forward against a pressure which wasn't the wind. If it hadn't been for Granpa he'd have turned back, but it wasn't only for Granpa's sake that he went on, it was for his own. What he needed was Granpa's company, the protecting intelligence that would drive away these stupid terrors . . .

Slowly the terrors lost their power, or his own reason began to work again. The gallery he was in seemed to be reaching an end. The air current was funneling through narrows, close to the floor, and the stream was making a new noise, a quiet gurgle, as if it was slithering down a pipe. A larger stream whimpered somewhere beyond. In a few more paces it became clear that these noises were rising from below, so Jake dropped to his knees and crawled forward until his fingers touched the ridged softness of an old balk of timber laid across the floor — another trapdoor. Of course, there must be a fault in the coal bed, which meant that wherever a gallery reached it the miners had either to stop digging or climb down to work at a new level. If there was a trapdoor there must have been a ladder. He lay flat and inched forward until his head and shoulders projected over the opening, through which the draft swirled up in wuffling eddies. He reached down.

Yes, a stout beam slanted down. A rusty rung joined it

to the wall. The gallery below ran to left and right and a fair sized stream rippled along it. Jake wriggled round to let his legs dangle and slowly eased his weight onto the first rung, gripping tight to the slithery framework of the trap-door until he was sure the rung was firm. Then, just as carefully, onto the next, and the next. Not far now.

His head was just below the level of the trapdoor when he suddenly knew that something was watching him.

His limbs froze. No amount of will could move a muscle, while his mind raced like a clockwork toy which has lost the part that is supposed to keep it ticking at an even pace. It raced, but got nowhere. What? Who?

Dave could have come up through the shaft again, found Granpa, followed the air current through the maze, turned the other way at the first junction, and now be standing watching him come down the ladder. The harsh beam of Dave's big torch might be on him now. But it didn't feel like that.

"Dave?" he whispered.

The whisper crept into silences. There was nothing there, no one. Slowly Jake's muscles unlocked, allowing him to finish the movement to the rung below. He was covered with sweat and shivering as though he'd woken from a nightmare, and his hand had gripped so hard at the beam of the ladder that he'd squeezed water from its surface and the drips were trickling down his wrist. Stupid boy, he thought. I wish Granpa was here. This sort of thing doesn't happen to you when he's around. It's just because you've been so tired, so scared, bottling all your fright down, and now it's come out like this. Get on with it. All you've got to do is follow that stream back to Granpa.

He started to scramble down the ladder just as if he'd been climbing on the solid bars of the school gymnasium, but three rungs down he trod into space. His left foot was already half off the rung above and his whole weight jerked suddenly onto the rung in his hand. The wood that held it ripped like wet cardboard. He grabbed at the next rung and missed as the back of his right ankle banged into the rung below the gap, tilting him out. For an instant he was free and falling, then the buffet of impact slammed into his back. He heard the air grunt violently out of his lungs before deafness and numbness closed in.

The "seeing" began while he lay on his back on the gallery floor. It wasn't the instant of fierce flashes that came with a blow on the head. It happened so slowly that he didn't really notice for a while. He was more aware of what seemed to be a huge soft weight lying on his chest. His legs wouldn't move. The air came into his lungs in croaking pain. I'm only winded, he thought. That's all. Winded. I'd better rest.

So he lay there, letting the jerking croaks turn to gasps and then steady into breathing, and became aware that there was color in his mind, very misty but shaped and unmoving. It wasn't like anything he'd ever "seen" before, neither the jagged flashes of pain nor the wandering vaguenesses of dream. It was all one color, and made him think of heat, so he decided it might be dull red or orange, streaked with black. It was arranged in a rough swirl, with more and stronger streaks near the edges and at the center a black hole.

It was a nuisance because it drove other things out of his mind. The strange, glowing rings, which were there whether he opened or shut his eyelids, seemed to insist on his attention; when he rolled onto his stomach and levered himself to hands and knees they seemed to move with him. That meant they must be happening inside his head. Perhaps he'd done something to his brain in the fall. He felt sick, and sicker when he staggered to his feet and leaned groggily against the tunnel wall. The fall had certainly made his hip much worse. He stood shivering for a few seconds, tried three wincing paces, and allowed himself to slide back to hands and knees. Crawl, he thought. Hello, the air current's stopped. They've blocked the shaft. Got to get back to Granpa. Not far now. Follow the stream. Granpa.

Back on his knees he found that the red rings were still there in his mind, more shaped and steady now. While he was wondering whether they might be connected with the damage to his balance he knew all at once that they weren't only in his mind. There was too much depth and distance; they stretched away like the receding drips of the galleries, with the outer rings somehow near and the inner ones far. The hole in the middle was just distance beyond. He was seeing a tunnel — not "seeing" but seeing. As soon as he'd decided that, he also saw that the bottom of the picture was different from the rest, flatter and not so heavily streaked with shadow. When he shut his eyes or moved his head from side to side the picture stayed just as it was. He didn't see more of either wall. Still he was seeing a tunnel, this tunnel, the gallery he was in. In the dark.

It didn't seem at all impossible or strange. Jake accepted it the way one accepts the impossibilities of a dream, though he was sure he was awake. He began to crawl painfully along the gallery, dragging his leg so that his hurt hip bothered him as little as possible. In a yard or two his right hand touched a raised ridge in the floor, running along the gallery, the remains of a wooden rail that had once carried the little coal trucks to the main shaft. Now in the picture he could see two faint markings along the floor which must be the same rails. Near the furthest end of them, deep in the glowing tunnel, he saw a movement.

It was all of the same color as the rest, but somehow more intense. He stopped to concentrate on it, but it seemed to have gone still so that he could barely make it out. He tried to listen for it, but his hearing was somehow muffled, or his brain wasn't working properly. Perhaps the balance of his senses was upset by the new problem of sight. He had lost confidence in sounds and echoes, and the ripple of the stream seemed to drown out more distant whispers. Irritable, he clicked his tongue against his palate.

At once the tunnel quivered and, without losing shape, receded violently. Jake thought that perhaps the picture was in his mind after all, and that the vibration of the click had shaken it out of place, but as he started to crawl on he saw the thing on the floor, further off now, beginning to move again. It was a small, rounded mass, shadowless, moving stumpy legs. He thought it was coming along the tunnel towards him.

A piercing shaft of excitement tingled through him, a sort of pure inquisitiveness, having nothing to do with his exhaustion or the danger he was in. It seemed almost to come from outside him and race along his nerves like an electric current. Yes, the blob was coming nearer, although (he now realized) his own crawl along the tunnel didn't seem to have anything to do with this. He could hear when he passed the entrance to a side gallery but he didn't see it happen. The walls of the tunnel — if that was what the red streaks were — didn't move or change. Now he could see that the blob did indeed have legs, two front legs, each with a joint near the middle, and two back legs, thicker and apparently jointless, but each trailing a sort of extra bit behind. It looked very clumsy.

This was near enough. Jake stopped, and at once the blob became still. Vaguely, beneath the surface interest and excitement, Jake was aware of something else, something not felt through his senses and especially not through this new strange sense of seeing, but still known. There seemed to be two Jakes, one of them watching the clumsy blob and the other one (who was really the same one) aware of another presence in the tunnel, a presence that had nothing to do with the blob, something quite different, quite different from anything Jake had ever known, a sort of tension, as sharp and definite as the smell of acid in a laboratory.

"Hello," whispered Jake.

Instantly the tunnel did its trick again, quivering, leaping away and steadying while the sound of Jake's voice still hung in the air. He didn't think the sound waves of his whisper had met any obstacle, certainly nothing large enough to fit the presence he had felt filling the gallery — filling, it had seemed for a moment, the whole of Annerton Pit. Anyway it was gone now, and there was the dumpy, glowing blob in the distance. Once again Jake felt the same shudder of electric fascination with it; and again, too, he felt the existence of two linked Jakes, this obsessed, inquisitive person who was doing the probing and seeing, and a more familiar Jake, very hurt and tired, longing to get back to Granpa but all the time being dragged into this unwanted, dreamlike adventure.

By now the first Jake's attention was so focused on the crawling blob that it took him some time to notice with his other senses that the gallery was changing. The stream a little way ahead had begun to run with more of a rattle, and the echoes came back from a wider space. Once he'd registered this he saw that the picture had changed too. It was the same at the center, with arching streaks surrounding the dark hole of distance, but near the edges the streaks had opened out. The floor was rough and tumbled. To one side, out of this roughness, rose an angular shape, which without thinking he knew was not important to what was happening now, a bit of old mining machinery, perhaps. It barely entered Jake's consciousness, which was fully engrossed with the crawling blob, and also with the large, strange presence he had felt before. That was there, bodiless, beneath the tingling surface of excitement. He was puzzled because he ought to have been able to feel with his hands the tumbled mess in the foreground of the picture, but the floor was just as before, smooth and slippery, with the rotted remains of the old track running steadily on.

He was beginning to feel that a trick was being played on him, that the floor of the gallery was somehow being made to flow backwards like a conveyor belt, keeping him always at a distance from whatever it was, however far he crawled, when the blob reached the edge of the tumbled area. At the same time his forward hand touched rock, with water trickling down it.

Down it.

The stream was running in the wrong direction.

The small shock of contact with the icy water became an explosion in Jake's mind. All his perceptions seemed to burst apart. He just managed to bite back the yell that flowed to his lips. The debris of that explosion in his mind settled back into new places. He found himself hearing the same things, feeling the same things, seeing exactly the same picture as before. But it was all different.

He wasn't seeing, he was "seeing."

The picture was happening inside his mind.

It was being put there.

There *was* something in the tunnel, a large, bodiless presence.

❖ 164

The tingling excitement was *its* excitement. The inquisitiveness was *its* inquisitiveness. The picture was *its* picture, which *it* was somehow putting into Jake's mind.

This glowing tunnel, this crawling blob were what *it* was perceiving.

The tunnel was Annerton Pit.

And the blob was Jake.

Those jointed forelimbs were human arms, those hindlimbs with the useless trailing parts were the legs of a crawling boy — a boy who had been crawling *away* from Granpa, *away* from the pool, *out* of the section of tunnel where the air current flowed, *against* the stream.

Jake stayed motionless for a long while. This was not the rigid trance of nightmare but a willed and deliberate stillness. He could see clearly now that the blob in the center of the picture, the glowing focus of the thing's attention, must be himself; but at the same time he became aware that this was only the focus. Somehow at the same time the thing was observing other parts of the mine, tunnels which must be far out of any line of sight; the whole maze was in its consciousness, and thus dimly in Jake's consciousness too; but all its attention was gathered into this one spot where a bit of old winding machinery rose gawkily from the rubble of rock that had fallen when the main shaft of Annerton Pit had collapsed in the disaster. Jake knew that he had come to the place where the miners had died.

He was afraid, but his fear was like his pain, something he must ignore now and cope with later. He knew the creature didn't like noise — at least three times it had leaped away — flicked along the tunnels in a single quiver of retreat — when he had clapped or spoken or clicked. It was timid, but that didn't mean it wasn't dangerous. Jake didn't know whether it could actually harm his body — it seemed to have no body of its own — but he had felt its touch on his mind. It mightn't know what it was doing, but when it had finished . . .

He willed a question, concentrating on that and nothing else, trying to push it out like a radio beam.

What are you?

He felt the response coming at him like a squall hitting a sailing dinghy. The mine seemed to heel and wallow under the blast of it. It came not in words or in pictures, not in ideas or knowledge. Just as the wail of a small baby comes out of it as a pure expression of its own hunger or fear or discomfort, without any thought taking place between the feeling and the yell, so the creature's answer flooded out of it. How did Jake experience it? At the time it wasn't like that. He was part of the experience, like a whine in the dinghy's rigging or a vibration in the baby's wail. But afterwards he thought that he had felt the answer with whatever sense it was that allowed him sometimes to feel things which didn't come to him through his bodily senses — things like Granpa's presence in the caravan or Martin's unhappiness. Only this sense was normally used for very faint signals. Suppose somebody has lived all his life in a world of very faint sounds, then if he is suddenly exposed to normal everyday sounds he will be deafened. In much the same way Jake was stunned by the force flow of the creature's being. It became unbearable. He straightened from his crawling position and put his hands to his face. At the first flick of movement the force flow stilled. The creature was still there, though, watching him, wary and thrilling.

He knelt for a while, trying to shiver himself back onto an even keel. Then again he formed a thought in his mind and pushed it out.

Too much.

❖ 166

It wasn't any good. The same thing happened, the same overwhelming blast of the creature's being, the same dazing chaos. This time he knew what to do and deliberately flung out an arm like a conductor stilling an orchestra. The blast stopped at once, but this time Jake immediately tried to echo back what he had felt. He allowed the echo to die, and waited. The presence seemed to withdraw, to contract. The picture in his mind became very faint. The drips along the galleries and the rustle of the stream were suddenly louder, and he was aware that his foot was throbbing with a steady, painful pulse. Then the creature asked a question.

?

It was like that. Not a question with any shape. Just a question on its own, like a note of music. But Jake knew how to answer because he had asked a question himself. *What am I?* he thought, and immediately tried to answer. Words were no good. It was no use thinking *I am a human being, a boy, lost, trapped.* He had to think sensations to explain what it was to be human, what it was to be Jake. He hadn't time to order his thoughts into any shape — in any case he was too exhausted to think that way. He simply allowed the memories to come: the taste of peanut butter thickly spread on warm white toast, while coffee made the warm kitchen smell like a shop, and Mum rattled at the stove getting Dad's egg just right; the thrum and hurry of riding on the BMW pillion; the shrilling of a school playground; lying on sand with the basting sun above and small waves flopping a few yards below; a rock concert — Deep Purple bashing it out and the fans screaming; the main road in the evening rush hour, with the churning traffic and the sense of all those people, each a little cell of his own concerns, going past in one solid tide; waking in a warm bed, feeling one's bones long and loose; Mum laughing; the baby next door crying; the sense of goneness when Granny — Dad's mum — had died; a picnic on Old Winchester Hill, with thin sun and chill clean air; pain; small worries; swimming; measles; laughter; homework; climbing a tree; fear . . .

The creature cut him short, echoing the remembered fear of an old nightmare of Jake's — one about being shut in a cupboard with a snake — with a pulse of terror, terror like an amplified drumbeat that vibrates right through the listener. Everything Jake had been trying to do, to think, to send across, was blotted out. He might have yelled. He didn't know what happened next. There was a gap, and then he was lying half across the wet rocks, dazed and sick. He struggled to his knees and realized that the creature was still there, watching.

Not only watching but waiting. Now it was Jake's turn. He saw it was no use making his thoughts gentle in the hope of a gentle response — if a voice only reaches you faintly you try to shout back — so he put his last energies into beaming the question across the cavern.

What are you?

The answer came strongly but not in that first impossible blast. There was very little in it Jake could grasp. It was like hearing music so strange that you can't even recognize that it's music at all. Pressure of rocks. Growth like roots along the shifting pressure lines. Waiting that wasn't waiting, because time wasn't the time Jake knew. A curious caution and wariness, as if the life that was fulfilling its nature in this way was somehow a frontier life. Other lives — not the scurrying crowds of Jake's experience, but few, remote, deeper, safer, known along fine tendrils of contact, all waiting through the time that wasn't time. Not simply waiting. Waiting *for* . . .

Then, as if in an instant, the pain, the wound. The

thing in the pit might have no body, at least not a body of animal cells like Jake's, but it knew about pain. Pain.

Jake returned to consciousness and found himself lying on his chest with his face turned sideways and water seeping along the sleeve of his anorak, but he felt too weak to move. The pain was over but the wound was there. The wound was Annerton Pit — these tunnels that led to the world of light, where the wind moaned through, scouring the maze with faint wafts of the living sea. The thing in the pit was powerless to heal the wound — it couldn't make one splinter of rock fall from roof or wall. That was not its nature. But it could grow its own protection, like a shell — a shell of fear, a barrier to drive back any creatures from beyond the frontier that might probe along the galleries of the wound and reach the central web of nerves where the thing crouched, aching for the old inviolable dark of its waiting.

That was a long time, but at last it changed. Something had come into the wound, a creature from beyond the frontier. There were others with it, but there was this one . . . It had moved through the maze, at first with others, then alone. It had crawled to this place. It was Jake.

There was a pause. Once more the creature asked its question.

?

(Are *you* what the waiting was for? Do you belong in this dark?)

"No," answered Jake.

His lips moved.

"It isn't dark for me," he said.

The glowing tunnel faded in his mind. The stream tinkled into silence. Smell died. Feeling died.

"It isn't dark for me," he whispered.

Then it was.

12

STINGING with fine rain the wind slashed steadily by. The BMW's engine seemed to like the wetness in the air, gnawing its way south with gusto. The tires made a whipping noise as they bit through the film of water to the concrete below. Other traffic flung up belts of spume — land spume, smelling of oil and dust, quite different from the salt spume of the North Sea. The cars that overtook them came past sedately, slowed to the legal speed limit on catching sight of the police car which was escorting the Bertolds home. On empty patches of road Jake could hear the swish of its tires and the purr of its engine right at the limit of his hearing.

The police had wanted to drive the boys home and ship the BMW down separately. They were scared of losing their prize witnesses in some silly spill, but Martin, trapped now in the machinery of a big trial, had been stubborn about this small patch of freedom. He would drive his own bike and Jake would come with him.

With his head tucked sideways out of the rain, huddled

against Martin's shoulder, Jake could sense his brother's misery and shame at the role he now must play, the accuser of his comrades, the tool of the very system that scarred the green hills, poisoned river and sea, murdered plant and creature, and spun mankind faster and faster towards destruction. Poor Martin, the official hero, the self-known Judas. He didn't even think that what he was doing was right. It was the result of escaping from Annerton Pit, and that had been right. But the rest, the chain of results that followed from that escape . . . Martin wouldn't talk about it. Jake thought Martin might still refuse to give evidence, but would that be right, either? The police had plenty of evidence without him, but by allowing himself to be a tool he might be able to show that the GR movement didn't have to lead along the road that ends with rows of the innocent dead laid out on stretchers in front of the TV cameras.

They had nearly begun on that road this time. It had been touch and go with Granpa, a doctor at the hospital said. Jake had spent three days in the hospital, recovering from what the doctors called shock and exposure, but they hadn't been able to give him the healing he most needed, a long talk with Granpa. Granpa had been too ill, too weak to do more than whisper, "Hullo, Jake," and listen for a couple of minutes while Jake explained that he himself was quite all right now. Granpa would do, the doctor thought, but Jake could see that it would be a long time before he'd be well enough to listen to what Jake had experienced in the pit, and explain it away.

Explain it away. Now, swishing south through the drizzle, Jake began to realize that no one could do that. Granpa might explain it but he couldn't explain it *away*. Inside or outside Jake it had still happened. When he had first realized the bitterness of Martin's misery Jake had begun to try to tell him about the thing in the pit. Suppose, Jake thought, he could persuade Martin that there had been something there. Suppose the something could affect people's minds. Suppose — not meaning to, but only as an instinctive defense — it surrounded itself with a network or shell of nightmare. In some people that would come out as terror, but in others it would come out as anger and violence. It would make them think and say and do things like Jack Andrews had done . . .

Martin had cut Jake short before he was properly started — he didn't want to be helped, not that way. Now, sheltering against Martin's back from the stinging wind of their drive, Jake was thankful he'd got no further. Gradually, without settling down to think it all out in an orderly way, he'd come to be sure that that was no way out. "Good" people can do "bad" things. Because they're good it doesn't make the bad things better — it only makes them sadder. And what they do comes from inside themselves. It's no use going into the deeps of Annerton Pit and finding a creature there and blaming it. If you mine down through the maze of your own being, perhaps in those deeps you will find the explosive gas of violence, the springs of love.

But the creature, the thing in the pit. Was *that* inside Jake? He called it a creature, but was it his own creation, a dweller in the maze of his being? How would he ever know? The more hours that passed, the further south they went, the less likely it seemed that it had any existence outside his own mind. He could no longer be sure that he wasn't inventing details. He hadn't once been able to re-shape in his memory the act of "seeing" the glowing tunnel or the crawling blob — himself — at its end. All he was left with was one last flutter of contact.

It had been the cry of a gull that woke him. The wind off the sea was shrilling between thickset twigs. He was lying in a sleeping bag.

"Granpa? Martin?" he whispered.

"They're all right, Jake," said a woman's voice. "How're you feeling?"

"Sergeant Abraham! Martin found you! Where is he?"

"Talking to the superintendent over by the cliff. He wouldn't leave you till I turned up. And your grandfather's in an ambulance on his way to hospital. You lie still. We'll have you moved away from here in a jiffy. How are things going, Mr. Cowran?"

For answer, veined down the threshing wind, came a new noise. Jake had heard it before, but only on TV and radio. It was an automatic weapon firing three short bursts. Close by, a man muttered into a walkie-talkie. A helicopter bumbled overhead.

"Stupid git," said the man. "We've got most of them, no fuss, but there's two or three holed up in a sort of shed against the cliff. Better hang on a bit longer, Sergeant, just make sure we're not in anyone's line of fire."

He returned to his walkie-talkie.

"What happened?" asked Jake.

"Oh, we were lucky," said Sergeant Abraham. "I was a bit worried when I got Martin's message about you going north of a sudden. Somehow it didn't seem like you. Then things started coming together, the way they do when police work's going right. I got a report of your granddad getting off a bus at Annerton, and when I wanted to send a man up here to ask questions my chief told me to lay off. I found your Mr. Smith, too, so we asked around Sloughby and Penbottle. Yes, you'd been there, but there wasn't any trace of you going north, where Martin said. It all stopped at Annerton, and the high-ups warned me off again. They were dead interested, though. You see, there's been a big police operation going on, looking for these people, and Annerton was one of the places we were interested in — not me, of course — I don't work at that level. But when I started putting in reports and requests they knew something was going on, and soon. We weren't quite ready to move, but we got a section up here disguised as a road repair team. So there they were, digging a dirty great hole in the road and pretending to like it, when Martin crawled out of the fields into their arms, with his face all covered with blood."

"Blood?"

"Just scratches. There's a thicket round the top of this shaft like you never saw. My guess is when they shut the mine they planted a thorn hedge round it and it's grown and grown. It took Martin half an hour to wriggle his way out, and it took our men that long to cut their way in to come and find you. We can't leave it like this. It's dead dangerous. The army is going to cave it in when we've finished here . . . Scuse me . . ."

The soles of her shoes creaked as she rose. Her skirt rustled away. Find me, thought Jake. Where did they find me? Martin would take them straight to Granpa. After that they'd look for me. Was I still at the bottom of the ladder, where I fell? Or did I really crawl to the main shaft? He eased a hand up to feel the chest of his anorak. It was musty damp, not soaking. If he'd really lain face down in the stream by the rock fall . . . It must have been a dream. Only a dream.

The man with the walkie-talkie was making quacking

noises of disgust and disbelief. With another rustle and creak Sergeant Abraham crouched down beside Jake.

"Listen," she said in an urgent voice. "Did you meet a man who called himself Andrews?"

"Yes. He was the boss. Why?"

"There were three of them holding out. The other two have come out with a message. They say that Andrews . . ."

He didn't hear the rest. His attention was blanked out by a sudden shudder of excitement, too fierce and brief for him to tell whether it was agony or thrill. That happened first, he was sure of it, just as he was sure that it came from outside him. Then came the explosion.

It reached him through the air and the ground and the mine in a confused hurl of noises and vibrations — one sharp, enormous slap followed by a booming rumble. A gust of heavy, dead mine smell whooshed into the clean dawn. The grumble of tumbling cliff drowned out the grumble of the sea. These noises ended, but still from below came the boom of falling rock. Somewhere down there Mr. Andrews, unable to kill for his cause, had deliberately died for it, and at the same time, not knowing what he was doing, he had begun to close the wound of Annerton Pit.

Dyingly the air moved up the shaft as the last compression of the explosion eased itself out of the maze of galleries below. To Jake it sounded like a whispering sigh of content.